Out of the Alley

Fiction Edited by Mark Koltko-Rivera:

A Book of Bryn Mawr Stories:
Annotated Edition
(Stories edited by Margaretta Morris
and Louis Buffum Congdon;
the whole annotated by
Mark Koltko-Rivera)

Out of the Alley

and other stories

Mark Koltko-Rivera

Seventh Street Press

an imprint of
LVX PUBLICATIONS
New York City
2014

Out of the Alley and Other Stories
by Mark Koltko-Rivera.
First edition, published May, 2014 by Seventh Street Press,
an imprint of LVX Publications, New York City.

Full Color illustrations edition:
ISBN-13: 978-0-6156-2952-0   ISBN-10: 0-6156-2952-0

Black-and-white illustrations edition:
ISBN-13: 978-0-6156-1906-4   ISBN-10: 0-6156-1906-1

U.S. editions printed in the United States of America.

www.MarkKoltko-Rivera.com   authorMEKR@yahoo.com
Follow "Mark Koltko-Rivera, Writer" on Facebook:
   https://www.facebook.com/pages/Mark-Koltko-Rivera-
   Writer/134875848276
Follow the author on Twitter: @MarkKoltkoRiver

Copies of this book may be purchased online at:
   http://astore.amazon.com/marswri-20

Booksellers: Check with your distributor for this book.

In memory of

Marilyn T. Pease

Manhattan,
New York City

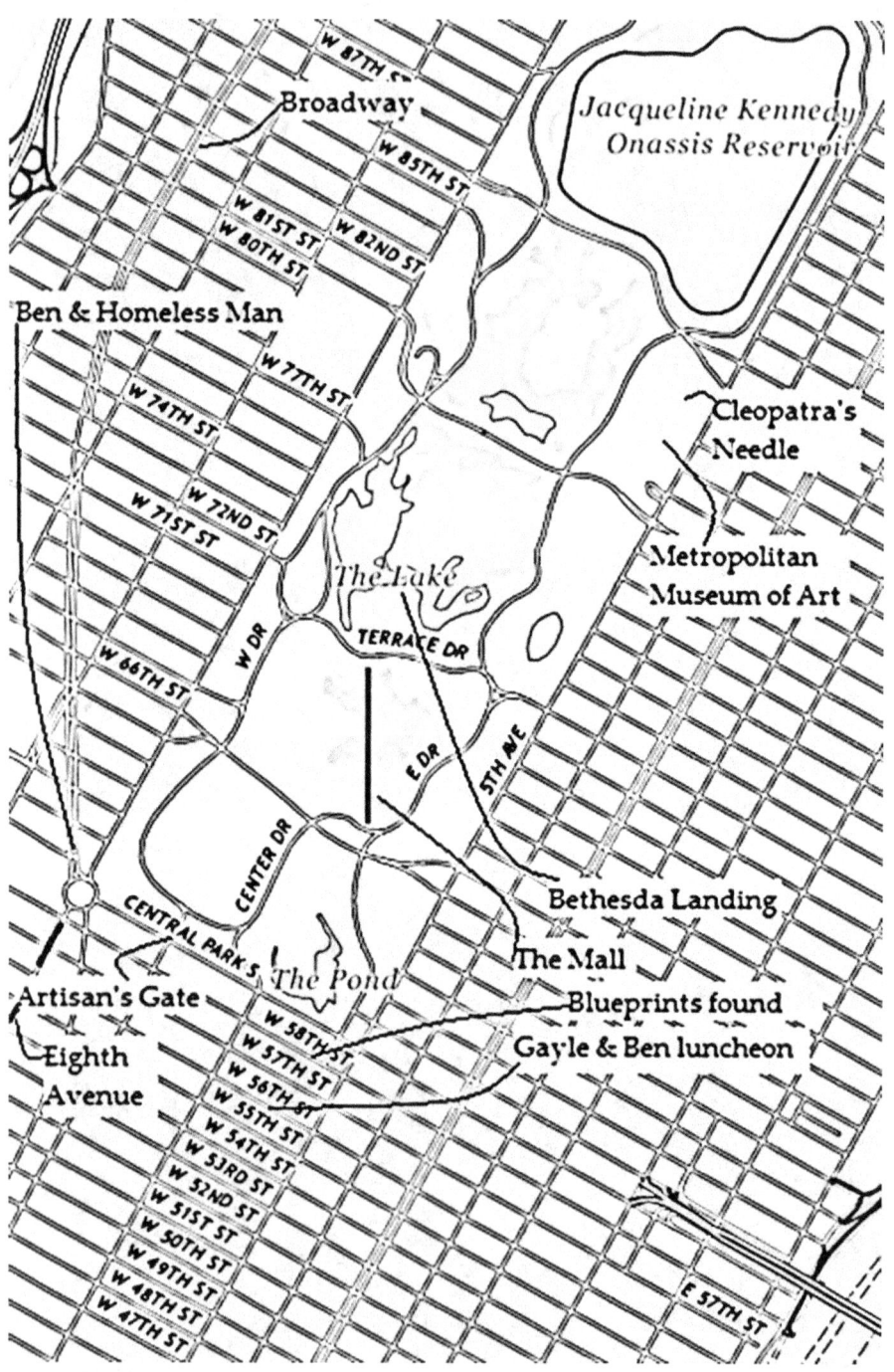

Contents

Out of the Alley

Spiritual Practice

CARLA HARTSHORNE CONSIDERED herself to be a good person. She contributed a percentage of her salary to the Mighty Way unified charities, and in the years when she was floor captain of the annual Mighty Way drive at work, she made sure her floor contributed more than the year before. She was thinking about this as she walked down Broadway from the Seventies towards her midtown office at *Progress Ahead* magazine. May had brought a change in the Manhattan weather and new charity campaigns to corporate America. Carla was angling for floor captain of the Might Way drive again. You got points for things like that with the editor-in-chief and the publisher.

Carla liked walking straight lines, but she took sharp angles and parabolic curves to avoid walking next to panhandlers. At one point, outside the church at West Sixty-Fifth Street, Carla dodged around three different panhandlers with strategic walking skills that would have done any wide receiver proud in the Super Bowl.

Carla was still congratulating herself for her footwork a quarter-mile farther south, when she noticed something that ruined her Monday in an instant: the sight of her lowest-grade editorial assistant, Ben Young, squatting on his haunches and talking with a homeless person. Again.

This homeless man, propped up against the granite wall of a building in the low Sixties, was in the worst shape of any of the homeless people that Carla had seen on Broadway that morning. He was fat, with longish hair so wild that Carla thought it looked like it could reach out and strangle passers-by. He wore pants with shredded legs, and a dingy tee-shirt crazy with splotches of food and vomit. *Ben Young is talking with a bum*, she thought. *Again.*

"I want you to hang in there," Carla heard Ben say. "Maybe I'll come by with a little lunch today if I can get away from my desk."

The homeless man mumbled thanks to Ben for a carton of orange juice as Carla stopped and stared. Ben looked up; he and Carla locked eyes for a moment. Carla turned and moved on.

Progress Ahead magazine published thoughtful, progressive articles for thoughtful, progressive people. Accounts of environmental crises, the latest trends in literature and the arts, the plight of the poor, scientific advances, political maneuverings, and the ongoing struggle for free expression and social justice filled its pages (along with one fiction and two poems per monthly issue). Carla was one of two associate editors, and her domain included features on social issues and the arts. The other associate editor brought in the essays that usually got the cover art and the major awards, pieces by the pundits and Jeremiahs of the nation. But that associate editor was approaching retirement, and so was no longer in the running for one of the senior editor positions that Carla coveted. She was sure that the corner office would be hers, so long as she kept publishing solid articles that brought in an award or two a year. But to ascend to the desk of senior editor, she had to look "editorial," in the same way that a presidential candidate had to look presidential. So did her staff.

That morning, after her usual Monday meeting with other senior staff, Carla called Ben into her office and had him close the door. She sat at her desk and waited for him to sit down. Ben was in his mid-twenties, over a decade younger than Carla; he was dressed in a style Carla always thought of as Older Prep Kid: khakis, blue buttoned shirt, a tie that showed color without bad taste, all pressed to the perfection of a display window. Ben sat down and smiled; as always, he seemed to expect the best possible outcome from any interaction.

"Ben, let me start off with a simple question," Carla said, gently and kindly. She stood up, bent forward, propped herself on her desk with her fingertips, glared down at Ben, and said "What. The living hell. Are. You. *Think*ing?" She sat down. "We are publishing professionals. We do not squat and chat with bums on the street. We do not *associate* with bums on the street. We do not bring *orange* juice to bums on the street. We do not bring *pizza*, *choc*olate bars, *mang*oes, or victuals of any *kind* to bums on the street. I never want to see you consorting with bums, beggars, or street people ever again, not today, not Tuesday, not any day that ends in the letter '-y.' Am I clear?"

"Yes."

"Then do I understand that you agree to these terms?"

Ben was silent for a moment. "No."

"*What?*"

Ben was slow and deliberate in his response. "What I do outside of work hours and outside the office is my own private life. There's nothing illegal or immoral about this. It's my business, no one else's," he said. "Not even yours."

Carla looked at Ben silently for a moment. "Get out of my office," she told him.

Carla sat alone in her office. The more she considered the situation, the firmer she became in her conviction that she had to do something about Ben and his bums. Due to the quirks of Manhattan geography, Carla and Ben *and* the editor-in-chief each paraded down Broadway to the office every morning, Carla from her co-op, the editor-in-chief from his duplex, and Ben from his pre-Civil-War fifth-story walk-up apartment. Broadway, the great equalizer. All Carla needed was to have the editor-in-chief see her assistant squatting with the homeless. The editor-in-chief was Choate, Dartmouth, a Rhodes Scholar, and old money. A sight like Ben and his bums would make Carla seem ... unworthy. But it was complicated.

Technically, Ben was entirely correct. His appearance, manner, and performance at work were impeccable. Unless he were busted for selling crack to fourth graders, there was little he could do on his own time that would allow Carla to discipline him professionally. Given that, a threat—all the more forceful for being completely empty—had been her tactic of choice. The threat having failed, perhaps she should resort to reason. But could reason succeed, where a threat had failed? Should she just drop the whole thing?

That night, as her lover started building up to his grand finale, Carla decided to go with reason to force the issue with Ben. Dropping the matter made it almost inevitable that her boss would see Ben sharing deli treats with derelicts. She had come too far to have her career derailed by an assistant.

She often thought of her career during sex. Her current lover, a trade press editor, was for Carla a step up from the editor at the university press who had preceded him, and so on. Her relationships were a different form of career development, all steps in building her relationship résumé, as it were. Someday there would be a marriage (to someone senior and powerful in his own right), a duplex, a tastefully raised child, a weekend place in the Hamptons.

We do what we need to do, she thought. He came. They slept.

Tuesday was all about setting agents in place. Next month there would be a big gathering at the Cathedral of St. John the Divine, an ecumenical soirée to celebrate the summer solstice. Carla tallied it up in her mind: There would be Wiccan priestesses, Tibetan Buddhist lamas (not the Dalai— schedule conflict—but local lamas from a temple in Ithaca, upstate), Creation spirituality Catholic brothers and sisters, two rabbis from Brooklyn, and a magical Qabbalist from Queens. The Cathedral was still looking for a Muslim imam who was interested, and had just scored one Shintō and two Hindu priests and a Jain. Sikhs were pending.

The editor-in-chief had decided to cover this event heavily for the September issue, for reasons known only to him. (*Intimations of mortality?* Carla wondered. This could be a good thing.) Carla had to rejigger her slate of writers to cover the event, after one of them copped the current all-purpose excuse—a critical family emergency—and another simply died unexpectedly. *These things never happen at convenient times*, Carla thought. By the end of the day, Carla had replacement writers lined up, and then she could think of other things.

Wednesday afternoon, Carla took Ben to lunch. Nothing like "21"; Ben was an editorial assistant, not a Nobel Prize winner. But not tube steaks at the umbrella lounge, either; they needed a place to talk. She selected a pub-ish restaurant and had them seated near the windows on the second floor, with a good view of West Fifty-Sixth Street.

Carla started her pitch after the waitress had brought their meals. "Ben, I'm trying to understand the whole chat-with-the-bums thing from your point of view." (Not that she was. But it was good to seem that she was.) "What do you think you're going to do for these people? I mean, my God, what is it that you see in them?"

Ben looked out the window for a long time before he addressed her. "Carla, what do you see out there?" Ben asked, still looking out on the street.

Carla glanced out the window. "I see West Fifty-Sixth Street. I see a bunch of TV producers, magazine editors, publishers and writers and advertising people and some tourists who look like they're lost. Plus a badly dressed beggar." And, she thought, someone who looked a lot like her lover, escorting some twenty-something skirt into another restaurant. There would be questions. "What do *you* see?" she asked.

"I see gods."

Carla paused. "Come again?"

"I see gods." Ben looked away from the street and faced Carla. "This is something my parents and grandparents taught me a long time ago. It's like, if we are all the children of God, then we each have the potential to become like God is: gods. Everyone I meet on the street is a god in embryo. They've just forgotten it." Ben turned back to look at the street. "Me, I just try to help them remember it."

"What, do you preach religion to them on the street?"

"Sometimes we talk about God. But mostly I just try to let them know someone looks at them like a person, and that a person is a very special kind of being."

"This is something you do all the time?"

"This is my spiritual practice. I call it, 'the practice of the presence of gods.'"

"Didn't I hear something like that in college? But it was different."

"You're probably thinking of 'the practice of the presence of *God.*' That's a spiritual practice from Renaissance France. You seek to feel yourself in the presence of God's love, all the time. It is an excellent spiritual practice, but my thing is different from that."

Oh, yeah—it's different, all right, Carla thought. "So, when is it that people become gods, then?"

"If they are good people, sometime after death. Long after death, I guess; I'm sure that there's a lot of training and education involved."

Probably not something the Learning Annex can help you with, Carla thought. "So no one becomes a god here, then, while they're still alive."

"No, not at all. I mean, we believe there are people who lead extraordinarily holy lives, who are taken up to heaven while they are still alive, but no one here is a god."

'We believe,' he says—there are more *like him?* Carla thought. *My God, the cults are coming back with a vengeance*, she thought. What else could these people believe in? The Sacrament of Sarin in the Subways, like Aum Shinrikyō? The joy of self-immolation, like the Solar Temple? Maybe just passing around the poisoned punch—the budget way to suicidal salvation? What color were their jump suits?

"So, Ben, what kind of—no, wait a minute." Part of Carla wanted to know what off-ramp religion it was that Ben had been raised in, so she could avoid it, but that knowledge came with a price. If she had to fire Ben someday, she was exposing herself to a nasty civil rights lawsuit.

She picked at her Cobb salad and considered how to proceed. The Empty Threat had failed. She could see that the Voice of Reason would do no better. *This guy might be hearing voices*, Carla thought, *but Reason is not likely one of them.* Then Plan C occurred to her: C, for Containment. What cannot be stopped can be shoved out of sight.

"Ben," she asked, "let me ask if you'd consider doing me a favor. When you come to work in the morning, and go back home at night—could I get you to walk on Amsterdam Avenue instead of Broadway?"

It worked well for about a week. Then came the morning when Carla saw Ben, squatting on his haunches again, passing an index card to the same bum in the food-and-vomit-covered tee-shirt with whom she'd seen Ben before.

"This is the address of the clinic," Ben was saying. "They told me they'd look at your leg for free. You might just need some antibiotics."

Ben looked up and saw Carla staring at him. Carla turned and walked away. Now it was time for Plan D: Deletion.

Ben dropped in on Carla's office in mid-morning. "Look, Carla, I came upon this guy over the weekend. He's sick. I just was telling him about a free clinic—"

"Don't worry about it, Ben," Carla said, without looking up from her planner. "I'm sure it all makes perfectly good sense. Sit down." Still not looking up from her planner, Carla pushed a piece of paper over her desk to Ben. "Here are some new assignments for you," she said.

Ben looked over the list. "Carla, these assignments—this deadline—I'm not sure ..."

Carla looked up. "Not sure of what, Ben? Not sure you can do it?"

Ben blinked. "I'll get this all to you on time, Carla."

"That's good, Ben. That's very good." *Fat chance, sucker,* Carla thought.

Carla had given Ben the editorial equivalent of the labors of Hercules to accomplish in two weeks, all of it in connection with the summer solstice celebration piece. Make contacts with new stringer reporters to interview religious teachers in Mecca, and the Al-Azhar University in Cairo. Arrange for someone to gather the reflections of the Archbishop of Canterbury. Find reporters who could get an audience with the Pope, and face time with the Chief Rabbi of Jerusalem. Put together in-depth interviews with a pile of people who were not so crazy about either ecumenism or the observance of the summer solstice: evangelical pastors in Georgia, Illinois, and California. Send someone to the outback of Australia to interview aboriginal shamans about their take on the solstice. Dispatch reporters in Rio to interview practitioners of Afro-Caribbean sorcery: the candomblé perspective. Did Polynesian villagers even notice the solstice? Did the Inuit have thoughts on the subject? Ben was to find out. And he had to get transcripts of the original interviews, translated into English, along with polished drafts of various pieces, onto Carla's desk—in two weeks, on an impossibly small budget.

Either he'll fail, in which case I'll write him up for dismissal, Carla thought as she watched a slump-shouldered Ben leave her office, *or he'll just run away. Then he can minister to his godlike bums all he wants.* Later, she overheard one junior staffer tell another that she had seen Ben at his cubicle, elbows on his desk, holding his face in his hands and saying

"YA-na-na-na-na-na-na-na-na-na-na-na-*naaaah*. YA-na-na-na-na-na-na-na-na-na-na-na-*naaaah*." Carla smiled and walked on. *Vegas bookmakers would lay four-to-three on Ben running away, then*, she thought. What she did not know was that, after four choruses of "YA-na-nas"—the world premiere of *I'm in the Deepest of Doo: An Anxiety Control Oratorio*, written, produced, and performed by Benjamin Young—Ben had taken a deep breath, sat up straight in his chair, and proclaimed to the universe and no one in particular, "And now the adventure begins."

For two weeks, Ben lived on fast food and diet cola, working twelve- to fifteen-hour days. In the first twenty-four hours after receiving his assignment, Ben was on calls around the country, South America, Europe, Africa, Asia, the Middle East, Australia, and several Pacific islands. He used Facebook and blogs galore to get journalism students all over the world to work for next to nothing. (*Who knew that the University of Alaska had a journalism program?* Carla thought later.)

An hour before deadline, Ben appeared at Carla's desk with three items: a pile of interview transcripts, a sheaf of pieces that Ben had edited himself, and a letter of resignation with two weeks' notice. "Ben, what's this about?" Carla asked about that third item.

Ben paused, considering the diplomatic response. "It's just time to move on, Carla. I'm sure you know what I mean."

"Yes, I'm sure I do. Best of luck to you, Ben."

Alone in her office, Carla pumped her arm in the air in a gesture of triumph. Then she dumped all of the transcripts and manuscripts into her trash can without a single glance at their contents.

Two weeks later, the celebration at the Cathedral of St. John the Divine was full of spectacle, singing and dancing and ceremony. Carla thought of it as a Cirque du Soleil for the soul. Although far outside of work hours, all the senior and many junior staff were in attendance. *One does not slight the Big Boss's obsessions*, Carla thought. Her favorite segment involved the Wiccan priestesses, their chanting and ritual dance, although she was disappointed that there were no spells cast to change anyone into an amphibian—*I guess it's just not the kind of thing these people do*, she thought. *A pity.*

The following day, the editor-in-chief had many of the principals from the celebration at a brunch-and-mingle at a rooftop garden restaurant near the office. Carla and senior staff were invited; the junior staff were not, but they had Ben's farewell party to attend instead.

This year, the precise moment of the solstice—the very second that the north pole of the Earth pointed most closely in the direction of the sun—occurred early that very afternoon. The Tibetans from Ithaca had arranged for their temple to bring in a five-foot gong to announce the instant of the solstice. Carla stood near the rooftop railing, looking down at the crowded streets of Manhattan, as the moment approached.

She had not slept well. She had dismissed the trade book editor a week earlier, when it emerged that his midtown lunches with the twenty-something skirt had been followed, now and again, by trips to midtown hotels. She was glad that Ben would be gone when she returned to her office, but yet, for reasons she did not understand, she was not fully at peace with this resolution. She looked down at the street, and remembered the lunch she and Ben had, and their conversation. She took off her sunglasses. The moment of the solstice arrived, and the Tibetans malleted their instrument.

>*Gong*<

With the first impact of the mallet on the temple gong, what Carla saw changed. The colors of the world became muted pastels, the boundaries of objects lost their sharp edges. What stood out were the luminous walkers on the street. Carla could see them down to the pores in their perfect skin, each individual eyelash of their perfect, glowing faces. They walked with bearing and grandeur, dignified movements that one imagined would grace a royal procession in Renaissance Europe. They were so very bright, brighter than the sun itself, yet Carla felt no discomfort in looking at them.

>*Gong*<

As one, the luminous walkers turned and looked up at Carla. There was love in their faces such as Carla had rarely seen between one adult and another; it was like the tender looks that she saw parents give to their very young children in Central Park, when no one was rushing anywhere and little Tony or Joanie was trying to gurgle out some word, or to make one small step on the child's journey. Then the walkers each raised an arm with an outstretched hand pointing to Carla, the way a Broadway star might gesture to an orchestra at curtain call. Carla looked at her own hands and saw that they were glowing; she, too, was brighter than the sun.

>*Gong*<

Carla fell to the floor of the garden restaurant. The wait staff helped Carla to a chair. She had not lost consciousness, but felt intensely weak for a few moments. When she was stable in her chair, she saw that no one appeared luminous anymore. Her editor-in-chief and other senior staffers came by to express concern, and Carla assured them all that she was fine—just too much time out in the direct sun, she said.

When Carla regained her strength, she left the gathering, fending off offers of escort, and went back to her office to look for Ben, who, she found, had just left his farewell party. *Must have passed him in the elevator*, Carla thought. She went down to the lobby, and out to the street, but it was hopeless; a three-minute lead on the streets of midtown Manhattan was as good as three hours' head start. Carla stood, looking at the crowds on Eighth Avenue, and saw hundreds of people, but not the one she sought.

Then she looked at the street itself. There, in front of her office's building, a patch of asphalt large enough to hold one person was torn away, as if someone standing there had been taken right up into heaven. Then a construction worker came by with his jackhammer and resumed his drilling.

Ben may not have been taken to heaven, but he disappeared as thoroughly as if he had. His cellular service was cancelled; mail sent to his old apartment address was returned without forwarding. On the Internet, Carla found dozens of people named Benjamin Young, writing and posting. She soon gave up trying to find him. After striving to drive him away, Carla thought Ben deserved his privacy and distance from her. She never spoke with him again. She did, however, have many conversations with the homeless and the hungry and the distinctly ill-groomed, conversations that occurred on most days that ended with the letter '-y.'

The Cryptographer

I CAN BARELY SEE the flowers and cards on the bedside table. They have placed me near the window, so when it is open I can hear First Avenue pretty clearly: the rhythmic roll of traffic, as the lights change; sometimes, as the hospital staff changes shift, I hear the laughter of staff members enjoying a joke on their way home.

Staff changes are also when I hear the occasional short beep of a car horn much more frequently. It took me some time to decipher what this change in signal was about. The taxis are honking at staff members waiting for the M15 bus headed up First Avenue; with the city budget cuts, there are fewer buses, so the Bellevue Hospital staff must be collecting in even larger crowds than usual at the bus shelters. The taxi drivers are hoping to drum up some business by honking the impatient staff. It's a gesture of hope, really. I imagine that sometimes it pays off.

The doctors have no explanation for why I am losing my sight. It started in my non-dominant left eye, and when I'd lost only half my sight there I was relieved to think that that was, as I thought, that. Then my right eye started losing vision. Now that the deterioration in my right eye has caught up to that in my left, they are both declining together, taking me with them into darkness.

There are better cryptographers than me, I'm sure, for whom blindness would only pose an extra level of challenge. They would continue to encipher and decipher in their minds, whirling their Platonic code wheels in the space of the spirit, beyond the need of paper, pencils, or certainly erasers. Their mindspace, no doubt, holds mental Enigma machines, where a code wheel encrypts each letter of a message with a separate cipher: for the first letter, "X" means "A," while for the second, it means "8." But mine is not that order of mind, and when my lights go out for good, there shall be no whirling code wheels for me.

I am but a lesser cryptographer. I have kept no state secret from our enemies' eyes. Mine has been the realm of puzzle books: at my height, *Crack the Cryptograms* was my playground, and I sold racy coded stories of spies, Mata Hari, and Maximillian Kuhl to *Coded Romances*. Lately, it's been all *Word Search Wonders*, and now, nothing.

Maximillian—never just "Max"—is my own invention, cool (like his name) on the outside, but passionate beyond all bounds within. I described his encounters—with NSA code clerks, MI6 operatives, and the occasional FBI special agent—in gloriously explicit detail. It's amazing what you can get past the censors when the hot bits of your story are encrypted, even in an easy-level letter-number substitution cipher.

I think my sight is a little worse today. When I got back from the MRI, I thought it was still morning, but I found out it was mid-afternoon, and light must be streaming through my westward-facing windows. It was all still pretty dim to me.

Charlotte did not come by this afternoon. I'm not surprised. She's a good-looking woman in her early thirties who still has options elsewhere. She used to tell me about the co-workers at the library with whom she had lunch, but that topic of conversation ceased to appear two weeks ago, although I doubt that the lunches have.

She used to tell me about what her family taught her when she was a girl in Boise, about how love could reach beyond time, how people could be married, not just as long as they both should live, but for all eternity. It is, as they say, a pretty thought, but it's been a long time since Charlotte has spoken of such things. I give her eternal love maybe as much as another week, before some lunch turns into dinner, the dinner into the walk home, the walk home into breakfast. And all because of my two failing eyes. (Yes, and all that that means, of course.)

Ah, the mysteries of love: file in a manila folder inside the larger green hanging folder labeled LIFE AND THE UNIVERSE, MYSTERIES OF. I used to think that I could solve them. I used to hope, secretly, that I could break the cipher of existence. For who better to decipher the coded messages of the universe than a cryptographer?

I tried first to interpret life in terms of straightforward symbolism, like a simple letter-word substitution cipher. See a dog in the street? "Danger!" That didn't get me very far, so I thought I should bump it up a notch, to the level of a true code, where a word might indicate a whole message by itself. In the eleventh century, a Chinese general would use a code based on the thirty unique words of a classic poem. Each word—say, "chrysanthemum"—would correspond to a whole message, like "need more food for my troops."

I thought that's what reality was like, one grand cryptogram. Missed my subway this morning? "Beware of missed opportunities." Dropped my bagel in the street? "You need to deny yourself."

It was interesting for a while, living in the world of Pure Code. But I never could tell what the words of the poem were supposed to mean. I finally saw that what I was doing was no more significant than a newspaper horoscope, so general that it could apply to anyone, at any time. My further attempts at the decryption of reality used more recondite approaches— Caesar ciphers; double-level puzzles; I spent weeks pondering nineteenth century French Masonic ciphers—but ultimately these efforts were no more illuminating. If reality's enigma is encrypted, there is some keyword I do not know.

Mr. Colón in the next bed speaks no English. His daughter Iris visits every day, bringing along her son Cristobel. Cristobel is seven, and bilingual. To give Iris and her father some time together, I play with Cristobel when they visit. He shows me his drawings, which I hold right up to my nose to see; they are boldly colored interpretations of dogs doing their business on fire hydrants, and I commend Cristobel for his unflinchingly realistic take on the world. I have taught him a couple of simple letter-substitution ciphers. Who can tell where this might go?

As for where things shall go with me, the news from France is not in yet, but I do not expect it to be good. I shall lie down in darkness, and one day soon, I fear, I shall rise in darkness.

It is night now, after lights out. Mr. Colón snores gently. The rhythm of the traffic on First Avenue never ceases. I can almost hear the code wheels spinning in the dark. If I tried very hard, perhaps I could make them stop in just the right position to tell me what all this has been about. But even then, I could not read them.

Out of the Alley

ON A HOT DAY in June, Ed stood outside a gated alley on East Fourth Street as workers unloaded a double-parked pick-up truck. Much of what they were unloading were Ed's belongings: hundreds of books, his convertible sofa with the swaybacked mattress, his broken desk and parts of his bookcases, the pieces of his *go* set, whatever Ed had not been able to bring over to his friend Anthony's basement storage units before the marshal had evicted Ed from his Seventh Street apartment that morning. Everything the workers had removed from Ed's apartment was being stashed in this alley next to the Fourth Street People's Theatre, to await a commercial trash pick-up.

It was strange for Ed, his hands in his pockets, to watch the workers haul his stuff—his issues of *Scientific American* and *TriQuarterly*, now all out of sequence, mixed together in big heavy-duty plastic trash barrels with his other literary magazines and the last five years' worth of the *Journal of the American Philosophical Association*, *Psychology of Religion*, and *Artificial Intelligence*. At first Ed wondered what the workers thought of this eclectic mix, but he saw that the men—this moving company from hell—were all recent immigrants from Eastern Europe. They had been hired off the books for cheap, and their grasp of English was poor. Ed realized that all his belongings were just garbage to them (although he did notice that none of his porn seemed to make it into the alley).

This is like watching my own burial, Ed thought. As he watched the interment of his belongings, sweat soaking through his tee-shirt in the muggy heat, it seemed to Ed that he had reached the absolute nadir of his life. Then his landlord appeared.

"So! This is it, huh?" the landlord said. "The end of the line. *Finito*. Man, I'm glad to have the two of you gone."

"The two of us?" Ed asked.

"You and the creep across the hall."

17

"Mr. Wynn?" Ed had barely even seen the man.

"Ah, yes, the wonderful Mr. Wynn."

"I thought he was on a trip or something."

"Yeah, some trip. Off to Lyons and Prague and a bunch of other third-rate garbage dumps. He sends me a letter from Rome—finally someplace decent—to tell me he 'must make a detour into Asia.' Who the hell has to take a detour to another continent? What, they block the road to Sicily with a big DETOUR sign, and the next thing you know you're in Shanghai? Who the hell does that?

"Anyway, he tells me he'll pay his rent with double interest when he gets back. No way to reach him and tell him, no, that's not the terms of your lease. So now *he's* out, *you're* out, and *big* surprise, I'm taking all ten apartments co-op, without having to offer insider's prices on two of them."

"He's lived there for years," Ed said.

"Yeah," the landlord said, "I know. And never a day late or a penny short on his rent. And you know what? I just don't care. A lease is a lease, and now his place is mine.

"And who are *you* to stick up for him?" the landlord continued, red in the face, and not just from the heat. "Way behind on rent, a grad student with a bunch of dead-end jobs and no degree in sight, who are you to stick up for him?"

Ed looked at the stained cement of the sidewalk around his cheap sneakers. This did nothing to cool down the landlord. The workers took embarrassed glances at Ed as they continued to lug a mixture of Ed's and Mr. Wynn's possessions into the alley, behind the landlord's back.

"Here!" the landlord continued, as he grabbed a box of books from one of the workmen, "He's such a good friend, you're sticking up for him? Here, have a souvenir of your friend!" The landlord tossed the box at Ed's feet, as Ed jumped to avoid having his insteps crushed.

"*Look* at this garbage!" the landlord yelled, as he rummaged through Mr. Wynn's books. "*The Whole Magician. Master, Mystic, and Mage.* Now *that's* a job title for you! Try looking it up sometime in the classified ads. *Walking the Paths of the Tree of Life*, oh, that's pure poetry. All a bunch of useless crap, every bit of it." The men brought the last of Mr. Wynn's possessions into the alley: an easy chair, a reading lamp, the curtains that had shaded his single window onto Seventh

Street, together forming a floating tableau of a living room that no longer existed.

"Maybe you too can wind up lying in the streets of Prague someday," the landlord shouted at Ed, "lying dead from hunger in the gutter, until they cart your body off to a pauper's grave. That's it! The Pauper of Prague! The Wonderful Wynn and the Pauper of Prague!" The landlord laughed at his own wit, and pushed Ed out of the way to walk towards Third Avenue, chuckling all the while.

Ed watched the landlord walk away, his own face now red with shame, the box of Mr. Wynn's books at his feet. He turned back to the alley gate as the men walked out, themselves embarrassed for what they had witnessed, poor language skills or no.

The foreman, a bald man with a beard down to his clavicle, was the last out. He looked at Ed with sadness, then turned to lock the gate to the alley. As he pulled the key out of the lock, he dropped his jangling keychain. He bent down to pick it up, stood up, and went to shake Ed's hand, keychain and all. "Goodbye. You good man," the foreman said. It was a bit clumsy for Ed, having the foreman clutch Ed's hand in a two-handed grip with a bunch of keys, but Ed was struck by the man's compassion. "Thank you," Ed said. The foreman turned to leave and jumped into the driver's seat of the pickup, the motor already running. He turned to Ed, gave him a wink, then faced forward and drove off down Fourth.

In his hand, Ed held a copy of the key to the alley.

People sing about springtime in Paris and autumn in New York. Nobody sings about summer on the Lower East Side of Manhattan, probably because it so often is either hot and humid or stormy. This was Ed's environment for the next few days as he used an old wheelie luggage cart, two bungee cords, and empty boxes for printer paper that Ed had begged from a local shop, to salvage as much as he could from the alley.

Anthony, a friend of Ed's since high school, worked for a large public accounting firm; he was glad to offer Ed the unused second bedroom in his co-op at the Village Garden apartment complex. Being often out of town on extended trips to audit clients—such as all of June and July this year—Anthony appreciated having someone around to watch his place. In addition, Anthony had two storage units rented in the basement, where he kept all of three cartons of old comic books, which he wanted off-site just in case he had a date over to his place. The rest of the storage space Anthony was glad to loan to Ed.

The bins into which Ed's stuff had been tossed had years of grime on them, ash and soot that got onto Ed's arms and hands, and thence onto his face and clothes. Since his mother had died, he had become casual about his dress, grooming, and hygiene. Now, with the filth of the trash bins on his body and clothing, and with him carrying his possessions on a damaged cart, his persona was complete: He looked the part of the stereotypical homeless bum, as he imagined his neighbors would say.

All the real thinking in Ed's labors was done in about the first fifteen minutes of each cycle, as he decided what he most needed to save from the alley on that particular trip (like personal notebooks, out-of-print books, and old photos). The rest of the cycle, about an hour and a half per trip, Ed functioned on automatic: he would pack his treasures as tightly as he could into the paper boxes, never putting more than three boxes at a time onto the wheelie; slowly lead the squeaky wheelie cart laden with boxes, Ed dirty and drenched in sweat, through a quarter-mile of the Lower East Side, his own Via Dolorosa, to the storage units, under one of the Village Garden complex buildings at Fifth Street, on the east side of First Avenue; go through the rigmarole of unlocking the outer door to the basement, the inner door to the storage units, and then the doors to the units themselves; stow the boxes inside a unit; and trudge back to the alley. As he came upon them, he also packed many of Mr. Wynn's books, hoping one day to run into him and return at least some of his books.

Flying on autopilot left Ed with a lot of time to think over his situation and how he had arrived there. Ed had always worked hard, but when it came to how to work smart, or even what to work on at all, he had always been left to his own devices. Ed's father had skipped out early and permanently, and Ed's mother, barely a high school graduate, was at a loss when it came to giving career advice to her son, highly intelligent but lacking in wisdom. At college, Ed had done excellent work, but he followed his wide-ranging interests by constructing his own major out of courses in philosophy, computer science, and religious studies. After graduation, he found that potential employers had a hard enough time knowing what to do with run-of-the-mill philosophy majors; present them with philosophy in a combination with computer science and religious studies, and their minds just ground to a halt. "On paper, you look like three people mushed together," one interview had said, looking at his transcript and résumé.

So this is one problem, Ed thought as he loaded box after heavy box onto his cart. *People think I lack focus. And maybe people are right.*

After college, his lack of employability led him to apply to grad school in philosophy. He handled the classwork easily enough, but then came the dissertation. Ed had futzed around for two years reading thousands of pages of material, just trying to get a clear topic that could be addressed in a single dissertation, "not three or four or five," as his dissertation advisor had warned him. Grad students without clear direction who are past coursework and comprehensive examinations find themselves cast upon an ocean with no shore clearly in sight. Some float along as ABDs for years, or forever, while others come to paddle in some single direction— perhaps pointed towards the land, or perhaps not.

This is another problem, thought Ed, as he trudged along toward First Avenue, squeakety-squeak, with his overburdened cart. *I not only need to decide on a direction, but I need to plan out my course of action, make my own deadlines, and keep them.*

His appearance among the storage units always sent the roaches and mice scurrying. These were deluxe, heavily armored, three-inch-long SWAT team roaches, too. Ed had spread boxes of borax on the floors of the storage units to keep the bugs away from his boxes, but still he was skeeved out by the sight of the things as they skittered away. At first Ed figured that the mice lived off the roaches; later he wondered whether it might be the other way around.

And now we come to the biggest problem of all, Ed thought, as he pulled his cart down the aisle between the storage units to his books' refuge. *I don't have Clue One about how to make these kinds of changes.* There being no air circulation in the basement, his perspiration poured off his head, dripping onto his eyeglasses, his filthy arms, and the boxes of books as he added each one to the grand pile already in the unit. *At this point*, Ed thought, *I need a miracle.*

Given the hours that the storage space was open, Ed could make four round trips a day. For three days he trekked in the heat and the rain, until he fell sick and stayed in the apartment all day while it thunderstormed outside. The next morning it was calm, bright, and cool. When Ed reached the alley, it was empty.

Several of Ed's part-time jobs had canned him simultaneously, due to the seemingly ever-worsening national economy; this had precipitated his eviction crisis. He made enough, tutoring undergraduates for the Graduate Record Exam, to pay for his food and some sundries; staying for free at Anthony's, Ed was free and clear in terms of cash flow.

The day Ed discovered that the alley was empty, and everything he had not stored was lost for good, he walked four miles uptown to the Metropolitan Museum of Art, wandered the Egyptian exhibits for two hours, sat down outside near Cleopatra's Needle, and cried. He caught the subway downtown, had some pizza on Ninth Street for supper, watched some of Anthony's cable TV, and turned in at midnight, which was early for him.

Late the next morning, Ed got up and went shopping. The week before Ed's eviction, he had benefited from some last-minute undergraduate test panic, which gave Ed enough money for a cheap second-hand desk and chair, a small bookcase, and a printer stand, his old furniture having been wrecked in the eviction. Ed spent the evening arranging his furniture, his laptop and printer, and some of his dissertation materials. The next morning, up late, as usual, Ed sat down at his new workspace, before a window looking out onto First Avenue over the Village to the west, from Anthony's spare bedroom. Through the open window Ed breathed in the fresh air, still cool. He would start over today.

Down in a storage unit digging around for his copy of *The Transhumanist*, Ed came upon the box of Mr. Wynn's books that his landlord had heaved at him, and some other of the volumes of Mr. Wynn's library that Ed had rescued. Examining Mr. Wynn's books, Ed recognized that they dealt with magic—the kind with visualizations and chanting, not card tricks. Ed gathered as much from some titles he could at least read, like *Numbers: Their Occult Power and Mystic Virtues*, a binder of some papers called "Flying Rolls," some bound issues of a journal called *The Equinox*, as well as from a title he could figure out, although he could not decipher the Latin content of the book itself: *Opus Mago-Cabbalisticum et Theosophicum*. A lot of Mr. Wynn's books were way beyond him—old, leather-bound manuscripts in Latin, Greek, Arabic, Hebrew, and other languages that Ed could not even recognize, one of them drawn in letters made of little circles connected with lines. Some of the printed books, of more recent date, seemed to be written for a more general audience. Curious, Ed picked out *The Whole Magician* to accompany him and his copy of *The Transhumanist* upstairs to his desk.

After spending most of the morning skimming through his notebooks in a fruitless effort to come to clarity on a dissertation topic, Ed had lunch out on Anthony's modest terrace, eating warmed-over pizza, and oranges that Anthony had left behind. Ed was stuck in the same rut he'd been in for two years: no clear idea for a project, and no notion of how to get one. He found himself repeating something he'd said on the Via Dolorosa: *At this point, I need a miracle.* But Ed did not think himself worthy of miracles.

Then he stopped working on his second orange, mid-peel: *Isn't that what they called magicians: Thaumaturgists? 'Miracle workers'?* With a speed born of desperation, Ed retrieved that copy of *The Whole Magician* from his shelf and spent the rest of the afternoon skimming it on the terrace.

The Whole Magician was basically occult self-help. As the author wrote:

> The magic is in the magicians. Thus, before attempting serious magic, the whole of their beings must be finely tuned instruments, their souls clean, their bodies healthy, their minds clear and diamond-sharp, their wills refined and strong, their emotions in balance.

The book largely consisted of a dozen lessons to strengthen budding magicians' knowledge of the esoteric, each lesson containing exercises to help improve the magicians themselves. There were terms with which Ed was not familiar—what was a sigil? or a boustrophedon?—but he got the overall thrust of the presentation.

Early that evening, after dinner at McDonald's, walking past the clubs on Avenue A, Ed thought about what he had read. On the one hand, the program laid out in *The Whole Magician* was attractive. Who wouldn't want to have a diamond-sharp mind? *Although that sounds like it could hurt*, Ed thought. On the other hand, it all seemed so focused on differentiating oneself from everyone else. Ed wondered, *What if this winds up being some sort of spiritual elitism?*

Ed passed the Zombie Cult Club as it was in full swing, packed with patrons dancing as if they had stuck forks into electrical sockets. People spilled out onto the sidewalk, with shaky balance. "*Man*, this is a great place," one stumbly fellow said, just before he leaned between two parked cars and evacuated what seemed to be the entire contents of his stomach. He looked dully up at Ed for a moment, and said, "Just skip the Brain-Sucker Specials. Unless they're *really* fresh."

Ed nodded his head in thanks for the advice. He wound his way back to Anthony's apartment. *Maybe a little elitism wouldn't hurt me*, he thought.

> *. . . their bodies healthy . . .*

Ed learned that the strength of his magic would be affected by the strength of his body. He began to patronize Wholesome Foods more often than fast food joints. He started going to the gym at Fordham—Lincoln Center, where his undergrad alumni status got him in for free. Ed slept better, so he got up earlier.

> *. . . their minds clear and diamond-sharp, their*
> *wills refined and strong . . .*

Ed found mindfulness meditation one of the hardest things he had ever done. The water glass on his desk could sit there and do nothing, but *he* could not, yet he kept at it.

By comparison, visualization was easier for Ed. He gradually formed successively clearer images of where he wanted to be, what his life should look like, and even what his dissertation should look like.

. . . their souls clean . . .

Ed never bought more porn to replace what he had lost in the eviction. Instead of this leading to increased sexual frustration, he found that life without porn helped him focus more clearly on every other goal in his life besides mating.

. . . their emotions in balance . . .

Ed learned about the Tree of Life, a kabbalistic design that, it was claimed, symbolized all of creation on multiple levels, including the human psyche. He began pathworking exercises, where he visualized walking from one part of the Tree to another, which was supposed to activate different 'energies' within himself. He met his mother and then his father during some of these exercises, and wept alone in his room after these encounters. Ed found out that, being a grad student at NYU, he could get several free sessions of psychotherapy at the university counseling center.

Magic requires precision . . .

Ed learned that magical workings—a pathworking, a ritual of healing or protection—was supposed to have more power if done at certain days, hours, and even phases of the moon. He started making daily, weekly, and monthly to-do lists and schedules, so that he'd do his magical workings at the right times. Then he started scheduling his dissertation research, too, and making lists of research literature to consult.

Magicians must then act in accord with their magical workings . . .

After Ed performed a working to bless Anthony with a girlfriend and prosperity, he cleaned the whole apartment and filled the fridge with fresh food. After he performed a working to further his research, he sat in contemplation for a few moments, taking notes of the thoughts that bubbled up in his mind, some dealing with his research, some with other, future projects. Then he spent hours in the library, following up on his insights.

The outer world affects the inner world, and vice versa . . .

Ed started presenting a neater appearance. He found he could get last year's fashion inexpensively at certain stores. The more confident man within wanted to look like a more confident man on the outside.

In six months, having received many referrals for his tutoring practice, Ed got his own place. One year after he started his magical practice, Ed defended his completed dissertation. Two years after, his first nonfiction book, *Of God and Robots*, was published to a front-page review in the *Times Book Review*. Three years after, he was beginning the tenure track in the philosophy department at NYU, dating someone seriously, and basking in the afterglow of being Anthony's best man at his wedding, while waiting for a check from the movie rights for *Of God and Robots*.

One evening, Ed sat on a bench in Washington Square Park with a nice angle on the Arch. Near him sat an older gentleman, quiet, yet with a poise like a retired business executive or professor—a master of something or other, to be sure. Ed thought he looked familiar.

All at once, the older gentleman let out a deep sigh. In a complete departure from every code of behavior regarding communication between strangers in New York City, Ed took this as license to ask what was the matter.

"Oh," the older gentleman said, "I have returned from a very long journey, to find that my apartment and possessions are gone. I've got another place, and there's not much I really miss of my stuff, but I did have some books I liked. It would take a miracle to find them again." And so Ed reintroduced himself to Mr. Wynn, with thanks for the loan of his books.

Art Form

SHE STARTED TALKING to me about a new installation in the late summer, just after school started. The budgets for the National Endowment for the Arts and the New York State Council on the Arts had both been cut deeply, again. Among other things, this meant that the downstream agencies which might fund undergraduate arts projects were essentially bust, so she knew there was no real chance that her own arts proposal would be funded. The company her father worked for had moved all their manufacturing to Singapore and folded their American operations altogether; this put her father out of work, a disaster to be sure, and it also terminated the company-funded scholarship program on which she depended, too late in the year for her to get financial aid through other means. She dropped out of Cooper Union, "temporarily," she said.

She explained all this to me while I was deleting viruses from her computer, or "de-worming the dog," as she called it. I did this for her about every two weeks, otherwise her computer slowed to a crawl and got qwinky; college student computers are the worst when it comes to such disorders. I saw that, since the last time I'd visited, she had taken down most of the hundreds of photos she had posted on her room's walls, pictures she had used to put her in the proper frame of mind for planning her "Legacy of the Sixties" project, which now would not be funded. Gone were the pictures of the Apollo landings, the Kennedy and King assassinations, Woodstock, Tricky Dick, the original Star Trek series, Altamont, Kent State, and choppers in 'Nam. She left up only a few images, and had repositioned those right above her desk: a close-up of a Saturn V booster at liftoff, the atomic bomb test at Bikini atoll, the buildings burning in Watts during the riots, a still from an early Virginia Slims TV commercial, a monk immolating himself to make a statement about the Vietnam War, some guy lighting up his draft card in front of a policeman, and a few other images that seemed to be random selections from her huge collection of shots from the Sixties.

"How did you pick which photos to keep?" I asked.

"Oh, just some favorites, I guess."

Favorites, right, I thought. I was just the guy majoring in engineering across the hall; I didn't pretend to plumb the depths of an art major's soul. But she was the sophomore younger sister of a pal of mine who was on study abroad in Rome, so I took on the elder sib stand-in role as best I could. At least she hadn't kept that creepy pic of the Viet Cong guy getting shot in the head by the police chief.

It seemed like she was trying to turn her setbacks into successes. Here she was, no tuition and no funding for her dream. So what does she do? She broods for two days behind a locked door, and finally comes out like a butterfly with a plan for a whole new project, a multimedia installation called "Destruction of Art / Art of Destruction." She described it to me as having two themes. One was the destruction of publicly funded art as a force, an effort dating back to the Reagan-era attacks on the NEA. The other was the idea of destruction as an art form in itself, particularly self-destruction. I thought this was a productive way for her to deal with her challenges. But how could she stage such an ambitious exhibition, being broke?

"That's the beauty of it," she explained. "All my artist friends at schools around the City are close to broke, too, so they can use this as a showcase."

"And the space?"

"My roommate's mother's company just went bankrupt," she said. "They've already cleared out a two-story office space in Soho, but they're paid up through the end of next month, so I can get my roommate to get her mother to loan us the space." It's amazing what you can do when everybody's broke and talented. Welcome to the New Normal.

"So what can I do to help?"

"Well," she said coyly, as she started to do the swinging-the-legs thing on her chair, "you *could* help me buy some paint." It was an utterly shameless attempt to little-girl me into laying out cash. Of course I agreed.

I did more than agree to buy her paint. I spread a fair amount of paint myself on cheap scrap fiberboard made into display pedestals; I set up tables, lugged a lot of stuff around, and so forth.

The installation was exhibited over the Columbus Day weekend, and it got quite a large attendance from both Soho and Village locals and the tourist crowd. She led me through the exhibit during the Sunday afternoon showing.

In the "Destruction of Art" section, we went through a gallery of what looked like abstract paintings and sculptures, all for sale, and all looking like stylized pointy mountain ranges, receding in the distance from left to right. Each one came with a sign explaining that it illustrated the downward trend of per capita arts funding, in different states and at the NEA.

The next room had theatre students re-enact legislators speechifying about cutting arts funding. Serrano's *Piss Christ* and Mapplethorpe's photos were raked over the coals again.

The final room of this section had a performance artist seated at a table. He had a stack of photographic reproductions (I would guess donated by someone's parent's company's color photocopier). This artist started with photos of classical Greek and Roman sculpture, at which he worked with scissors to cut out areas surrounding breasts or genitals, male or female, even when clothed—that, and eyes. Then he moved on to Renaissance artwork, slicing up Da Vinci and Dürer. He chopped his way through the last four centuries of Western art, amassing piles of snippets and mutilated art, until finally he was cutting into what looked like children's drawings from off the refrigerator doors of America. At the end, he swept all the scraps into a large trash bag and left the room with his scissors. A group of artists in rotation performed this twenty-minute piece twice an hour.

We began the "Art of Destruction" section on the upper floor, entering a gallery of videos showing building implosions at demolition sites across the United States. I had lugged in most of the TVs myself, unloading them from cabs as the artists lent their own equipment to the installation. A video mix of the implosion recordings was offered for sale. "All off the Internet," she whispered to me.

We entered a room of actors engaged in various acts of self-destruction. Smokers stood out on the fire escape, coughing and arguing for the concentration-enhancing effects of tobacco. A screen played the film *Requiem for a Dream.* Several actors sat at card tables with bottles of brand-name gin, whisky, and vodka, seeming to drink themselves into a coma as they talked about alcoholic artists, writers, and actors. "How'd you get the hooch?" I asked.

"It's water and flat diet ginger ale in washed-out bottles," she replied. "These people have to perform this act for three days running."

"Not to mention, booze ain't cheap, and half these people are underage to drink in New York."

"Not to mention."

The last "gallery" of the installation was the top of the building itself, where a roughly circular platform had been built out of three layers of cinder blocks. Bags of shredded art, the remains of the victims of the scissor-wielding performance artists, stood off to one side.

"Tomorrow," she explained, "we're going to burn the torn Body of Art as a sacrificial victim."

"How did you ever get a fire permit for this?"

"Hmm. 'Fire permit.' Interesting concept."

"Oboy."

"Yeah. I'll be thinking hard about that."

I had not planned on coming down to the Soho installation for the final Monday showing. After some study and a session at the gym, I was in the shower when her call came. She left a message:

> "Hi, it's me. My roommate is home with a bad cold. Please look in on her, and let her know I love her, and ask her to let you into my room, where you'll find the receipt for the paint propped up on my computer. Also, something else. You have been a real doll through everything, not just the installation, but everything over the last several months. I want you to know that I'll always be grateful for that. 'Bye."

It was an odd message, because I was going to take her out to dinner in a few hours to celebrate her installation, and she would have plenty of opportunity to speak with me in person. However, I did as I was asked. I brought some chicken soup to the roommate and discussed with her the relative benefits of various over-the-counter and home cold remedies. Then I had her let me into my faux little sister's room.

It was the neatest I had ever seen it, a cover shot for *Responsible Art Student Lifestyles*, paints and supplies neatly stacked, clothes stowed, trash collected and discarded. In short, this was nothing like her room's usual condition. What I found strangest was the condition of her bookcase: at least half of its contents were missing, including not only all her library books, but a lot of her personal collection, as well.

Propped up on her computer was the paint receipt. I was about to fold it up and walk out when I noticed one line item: two gallons of "Fire Engine Red." That also was odd, because I had seen no red anywhere in the installation, other than some of the paintings in the first gallery, and some of the reproductions attacked by scissors, and all those had been created by other artists. Everything I had painted at the installation had been utilitarian white, for pedestals and the occasional wall touch-up, paint fully accounted for on the receipt. I sat at her desk, looking around the room, and I saw almost nothing red, except for some of the pictures from her aborted Sixties project, posted above her desk.

Something about those pictures caught my attention in a way that they had not, during the weeks I'd seen them there before. Nuclear fire. Rocket engines' fire. Buildings on fire. A cigarette and a draft card on fire.

Fire Engine Red.

Fire *Extinguisher* Red.

The monk on fire.

I ran out of the apartment without closing the door to her room.

From people who were at the final showing of the installation, as well as the newspaper articles that followed, I learned what happened. At the closing event of the installation, after the sold paintings had been handed over to their buyers, she had gone to the rooftop platform of cinder blocks.

She had been dressed in a gown, simple and white like a nun's robe, or a shroud. She addressed the crowd of onlookers without notes:

> "Across the ages, much of the best art of the West has been produced under patronage. Princes, popes, and the people themselves have all commissioned or funded some of the best painting, sculpture, dance, drama, poetry, and storytelling the human race has ever created. Now that public patronage is disappearing, perhaps all that is left for artists is to make works of art from their own self-destruction."

She walked onto the middle of the cinder block platform, which was covered with the shredded scraps of artwork left by the performance artists. Sitting down, she pulled out from under the shreds a container of gasoline, which she poured over herself. She pulled out a lighter taped onto the gas container, and set herself aflame.

People went running for fire extinguishers. They found cleverly painted but nonfunctional replicas, attached to each of which was a key and a note stating that the real extinguishers were placed in the basement in a locked cabinet, which could be opened with the key. By the time people got to the basement and returned to the roof with the extinguishers, she was gone, as she must have planned. EMTs declared her dead at the site. By the time I arrived, the police had already cordoned off the site and taken her body away.

The NYPD detectives interviewed everyone having any connection with the installation, including me. For a while they were concerned that her suicide might have been some reaction to the breakup of some hypothetical romance between her and me; I told them that this would be a big surprise to my boyfriends, and after some more interviews that line of inquiry was dropped. Ultimately, the detectives confirmed officially what her friends had figured out: she had made all her preparations in secret, and alone, and had exhibited no obvious advance sign of her plans.

She had placed a video camera on a tripod with a clear view of both her brief speech and the cinder block platform. The camera fed into a streaming video, archived into a downloadable file on her blog—an arrangement I had created for her. Before her website was shut down, the video had already gone hyperviral internationally, which no doubt was her hope. It has been played for Congress and in statehouses around the country, Canada, Europe, and elsewhere. The effect that this video ultimately will have on legislators and funding agencies, if any, is unknown as I write this. I thank God that no one has emulated her piece of performance art.

What she did was wrong, period. Under the worst of circumstances, she should have followed the first imperative—survive—and lived to create her art some other day. Maybe she thought she was being considerate—putting a fire retardant mat under the cinder block platform, returning her library books and giving away many of her own—but she ignored the effect her act would have on others, as, I have learned, so many suicides do. The suicide of one of her siblings that winter, and her father's subsequent breakdown and death, can both be laid at her charred feet. But what she did was borne out of hopelessness, and possibly a depression that none of us detected, as well as the desire to give herself for a cause beyond herself. I think I understand what she did, even as I vigorously reject it.

Two days after she died I received a note that she must have mailed just before she went into the installation's final showing:

> By now all will have been revealed. I am sorry that I cannot make it to our dinner appointment. I am even sorrier that I have had to keep all this from you, but you would stop me, like a good friend should, and this is something I feel I have to do. I hope that this makes some kind of difference.
>
> If perchance you come upon some poor artist out on the street with something to sell when you have some extra bucks in your pocket, please consider picking something up. You may not be a Medici, but you too can be a patron of the arts.
>
> Thank you for everything.

She signed it with "Love" and her name. I keep this note in a lacquered box with a Tree of Life design that I bought from a crafts artist on Washington Square during the following Spring show. It looks nice on my dresser, next to the paintings and photographs that follow me home from time to time.

The Gondolier of Bethesda Landing

IT WAS ON THURSDAY, September eighteenth, that she decided to take a Walk.

She always thought of an occasion like this as if it had an initial capital, and so was a Walk. Several times a year, when the unease in her soul was especially turbulent, she took a Walk, to try to gain clarity or, at least, to negotiate a working arrangement with herself. Her younger brother had once observed that these Walks were not randomly distributed throughout the year, but rather were aligned with solstices, full moons, equinoxes, or some such. However, she had never paid attention to the rhythms of sun, moon, or earth. She did notice when the inner nagging became too heavy to ignore, and that's when she took a Walk. Six o'clock this morning was such a time, and she took this Walk at the south end of the park, entering at the Artisan's Gate off Central Park South and Seventh Avenue.

At first she thought of work, which was her typical way of avoiding what a Walk was all about. She found no refuge there. Her business responsibilities were all in order. At thirty, she had successfully brought into the agency accounts for an airline, an automobile, an oil company, a consumer electronics firm, and more, over the course of only five years. Interns and new hires believed her to be a minor angel. Upper management at the advertising agency, who well knew the unstable financial realities of the sea upon which their fortune sailed, dropped the "minor" from that description.

Her saves in the line of duty were stories of legend. Pitching a vodka account in L.A., ever-cautious she had flown into town on Saturday for a Monday afternoon meeting. The agency's creative head and media director, trying to fly in on Sunday, both wound up stuck in O'Hare when wind conditions became perilous. She had run the entire presentation solo, got the business, got their whiskey *and* bourbon *and* champagne accounts as well, and increased agency billings by seven percent, single-handedly, in one day.

This was not a morning for a Walk at the Pond, she decided. She walked briefly along the paths bordering the roadway, filled with joggers and bicyclists speeding past her on a road soiled by the horses that drew carriages for hire. She wished to shout out at the exercisers, *You are breathing horse dung deep into your lungs with every step*, but she knew that those kinds of straightforward messages were seldom appreciated, even by those who needed them most. To motivate them to change their ways, she thought, they would need to be hit by the psychic equivalent of a two-by-four, or a nasty lung infection, not by some mere statement. She headed for a place where the carriages could not go, where she would breathe deeply and think.

Pitching a Japanese electronics game account during a trade show in Boston, she had dragged in her younger brother, the unemployed 'writer,' longtime game freak, and former missionary in Japan; she had bought him a haircut and better clothes. His language skills and dopey little tales from the mission field won over the famously reserved clients. As a missionary in Hiroshima, her brother had once mispronounced two syllables of a 38-syllable sentence; thus, instead of saying that the resurrected Jesus had a tangible body like a human being, he had solemnly testified that the Lord had an edible body like a carrot. After hearing this particular story, at least one of the Japanese executives had soiled himself laughing. She bought her brother three new game systems from her bonus money. And a car.

She was resourceful, driven, loyal, quick-witted, and brilliant. She was also deeply unhappy, for reasons she could not articulate; hence the occasional Walks.

She reached Literary Walk, that stretch of the Mall where statues to some of literature's immortals had been placed. It bothered her how short Literary Walk was. Shakespeare and, oddly, Columbus flanked the entrance to Literary Walk, but then there were only three other statues, one each to Sir Walter Scott, Robert Burns, and Fitz-Greene Halleck. Put aside the fact that these were the very Whitest of Dead White Men. (*Not even Dante*, she thought.) *How the hell did Halleck make the cut?* she wondered. Halleck was a bad poet and a cranky satirist, productive for just a few years. She would have put a lot of money on a bet that ten randomly selected professors of

American literature could not put together three meaningful sentences about Halleck's verse. And yet, U.S. President Rutherford B. Hayes and his entire Cabinet had attended the dedication of Halleck's statue, a larger-than-life bronze on a monster granite pedestal.

She figured that there was room for seven more widely spaced statues along Literary Walk. She used to go over lists of possible candidates, until finally she realized that she was always stuck on the last one—because she wanted it to be her. But no one erected statues to advertising account executives, no matter how large their billings.

Literary Walk was the southern end of the Mall, one of the few features in Manhattan aligned along a true north-south axis. As she walked north, past Literary Walk, under the arch of trees just beginning to lose their leaves, she could almost feel the sun rising, directly off her right shoulder.

Passing the northern border of the Mall, she turned east and stood before the sad, gently crumbling Naumberg Band Shell. She saw herself there, on the stage, speaking, saying something with passion and conviction and inspiration to an unseen audience. But she could not make out her own words. Something about nuclear disarmament? And the environment? Minority rights? Affordable housing? She could hear intonations and emphases, but few syllables.

Returning to her northward course, she crossed a road, and stood looking down upon the magnificent Bethesda Fountain and Landing, on the Lake. Some considered this the very heart of the Park. A broad brick plaza led to steps that went right down into the waters of the Lake. (She thought she remembered boats picking people up on those steps, when she was a little girl.) In the center of the plaza stood a three-story fountain, splashing away even now, topped by a huge statue of an angel in a position of—what? Calming? Healing? Something soothing.

She took a deep breath of fresh air as she took in the scene. At the east and west ends of the quay on the Lake, the parks commission had placed tall ornate banners like something out of Lord Dunsany, Tolkien, or Eddison: an orange one with the seal of Parks, and a green one with the seal of the City.

As she came down the stairs and crossed the plaza to the edge of the water, she thought it would be fitting to see a barge landing there, with a delegation from the High Warden of the Esanocian Marches, dressed in ermines and jewels. Instead, she saw a gondolier.

He was dressed simply, in black trousers and a white poet's shirt, light on the frills but big on chest hair. His gondola pole was scarlet, and his gondola, unlike the style in Venice, was a cool spring green. He brought his gondola to rest just a foot or two beyond the last step of the quay. She noticed that, like her, he wore no ring.

"Could I invite my lady on a journey?" he asked.

"Where are you going?"

"To a place much like this, where nothing is the same."

"Hmm?"

"We share the same sun and moon, but we have no appointments, no promotions. We enjoy each day like a finely cut gem."

"Sounds self-indulgent."

The gondolier laughed. "Oh, really?" He said in a gently mocking tone, "And what has all your self-denial and discipline gotten you?" He smiled, and turning his gondola, poled a course to the west of the Lake, around a bend and out of sight of the Landing. She stood on the quay for a long while and then slowly walked to the office, as she had planned. She sat in her office for some time, her assistant holding all calls.

On Friday morning, she was back at the quay. It was not long before the gondolier came by. "So, how does my lady this morning?" he said.

"I am wondering just who or what you are."

"I am but a simple gondolier, my lady."

"No, you're not."

He laughed again. "My lady sees through my thin disguise. Call me, then, an agent provocateur of the soul. A gadfly. A cosmic noodge. I am a rogue tarot card, the Ace of Gondoliers, and your task is to find the best interpretation of the Mystery that I present."

"You are a temptation."

"And how does my lady deal with temptation?"

"I never submit to it."

"Oh," he asked, smiling, as he started to pole his gondolier away. "Haven't you now?"

She stood again at the quay, watching him leave. The walk south on the Mall was slow—or was she just thinking even more quickly than usual?—as she pondered what the gondolier said. She had taken the safe route in her life, the path to financial security above all else, the economics degree followed by two years in business followed by Wharton followed by five years in driven pursuit of success at the agency.

She came to the pitifully scant Literary Walk. Her sloppy younger brother, the 'writer'—with his lousy apartment and crapulous job, all on a corner of Staten Island—at least he tried to be true to some sort of vision, with his pitiful little stories and the four novels he was always working on. (Never the same four, from one family holiday to the next; just, four.) He needed her help with the rent from time to time, but at least he aimed for something beyond himself. She realized that, if Indulgence was a temptation, so was Security, a false idol of which she was a fervent devotee.

She walked to her midtown office, arriving the first of all staff, as usual. By the time her assistant arrived, she had written a memo directing him to postpone a number of her appointments, and describing which sorts of calls she would and would not be available to accept throughout the day. She had planning to do, as she considered her accounts and her many responsibilities. By the end of the day (she being the last to leave, also as usual), she had a new prioritized to-do list for each account, and a calendar of new goals to accomplish over the next two weeks. She pursued different phases of planning through the weekend at home, as she consulted her personal financial statements and online course catalogs, and composed what amounted to a cross between a personal business plan and an order of battle.

Early Monday morning, she returned to the quay. It was not long before the gondolier poled his boat to a position just off the steps into the water.

"And how does my lady do this fine morning?" the gondolier asked.

"Very well, actually," she answered. "And yourself?"

"Oh, if you are doing well, then I am in extraordinarily fine condition. And what leads you to this happy state?"

She sat down on the top step of the quay, her sensible shoes just inches above where the water lapped on and off the bottom step. "I've decided to make some changes," she said. "I won't be taking your gondola around to the other side of the Lake, but I won't be continuing the journey I've been taking either."

"How so?"

"I'm leaving the agency. 'Pursuing other interests,' they call it." She described her plans to him: the blogs and the opinion columns; the master's degree in political science, the public access television show; later, after she had garnered some publicity, the radio show, working off her contacts in broadcast media. Maybe law school.

"And your ultimate objective?" the gondolier asked.

"To make a difference," she answered, "for something more than what brand of toothpaste someone buys."

The gondolier smiled, nodded, and started to pole his gondola away from the quay. She stood and said, "Sorry I won't be taking that journey with you."

"Oh, aren't you, though?" he replied. She watched him pole away to the west, until he floated out of sight.

Six and a half years later, she was back at Bethesda Landing, standing just north of the fountain, facing a magazine of photographers and reporters and the Lake beyond, as she announced her candidacy for the State Assembly. Photographers were on their knees and in limbo positions, straining to get the shot of her with the angel of the fountain high in the background.

"Centuries ago," she said, "so the story goes, an angel came down to disturb the waters of the pool of Bethesda in Jerusalem." She gestured to the angel on the fountain behind her. "Whoever then stepped into the pool first was cured of whatever illness they had.

"Maybe there are still angels out there healing the sick. But for the most part, we have to be our own angels. We have to be angels for better prenatal care, better mental health care, better care for the poor with AIDS and veterans with traumatic brain injuries . . ." She outlined her platform with enthusiasm, and when she saw the gondolier, gliding out on the Lake far behind the press corps, she returned his nod.

The Death of Mozart

AFTER SHE DIED, her obituaries appeared in the New York City papers. All of them mentioned her time on the Lower East Side; none of them happened to mention her specific former address on Seventh Street. On the day her obituaries appeared, I walked over to No. 85, just west of First Avenue, a couple of doors from the bar called Bar. I saw that the current occupants of my old ground-floor studio had placed wind chimes between the blinds and the glass on the interior of the window; perhaps they opened the window sometimes, or maybe the chimes were just a useless accessory.

There were no mourners gathered in front of the place, of course. If any there were, they would be outside her place in L.A. But the mourning of rock stars is a New York thing; in L.A., she'd become a stop on the Dead Stars guided bus tour, so instead of mourners she would have gawkers. There were none of those on Seventh Street, either, and no crepe hanging from the second-floor window where she had once rented an apartment in the front. The occupants there probably did not even know she had lived there, might not even recognize her name. I had called that name out, some nights, long ago, right up in that second-floor apartment.

In '79 I had moved back to the Lower East Side from Jersey after my first marriage broke up. The first-floor front studio was shaped like a bowling lane, but it was mine.

Two months and another tenant's heart attack later, I saw someone moving into the second-floor front apartment and offered to help. She was tall and painfully thin, possessed of an energy just this side of manic, and, perpetually, a pack of Marlboro's, as well as short spiky hair obviously bleached blonde. Her accent suggested that she was from somewhere down South, but she was always vague about her origins. Her mom was in one place, dad was in some other, and quasi-siblings of various degrees of consanguinity were sprinkled from Charlottesville to Miami, New Orleans to Savannah, in a crooked sign of the cross over the Southeast. It was a little weird hearing her call me "honey" when we'd just met—"honey, pass me that box cutter, would you please?"—but I recognized this as a Southern thing.

She was the lead singer of a band called The Awful Wrath. She and her band mates had pooled cash, liquidated inheritances, and cleared out a minor trust fund to move to New York to try to make it on the still relatively new punk rock scene. They rented rehearsal space by the hour in the unused portion of a warehouse on Thompson, and played clubs all over the Village.

Their music was—dare I say it?—vicious, kinetic, and very loud. "Hunt That Liar Down" was a crowd pleaser, especially among the ladies. "Beat The Rich With A Stave" was more of a favorite with the gentlemen.

She was the center of it all. It was not just that she wrote most of the songs herself. Onstage she was a gasoline fire in black leather, not just singing words, but declaring them in screams with the voice, and staring with the eyes, of a mad goddess on a very dark night of the soul. I came out of The Awful Wrath's first New York show, a gig at the old St. Mark's Bar and Grill, feeling that I'd witnessed the birth of a new breed of demon.

That first night, after the last set, most of the band had to start a late drive to Georgia. Somebody's uncle had just died in a knife fight at the Sunday School picnic, and they were off to the funeral. She wasn't going because she'd had some kind of unfortunate "experience" with the newly knifed man. I volunteered to help lug things to the truck so they could get an earlier start, and then I walked her home and up to her apartment.

The next morning at breakfast, she seemed a very different person from her onstage persona. We were at that apotheosis of Lower East Side diners, the Kiev on Second Avenue and Seventh Street, a 24-hour place that could feed an entire Polish *shtetl* and still have room for a bus of old beatniks and two vans of Deadheads, and feed them all whatever they wanted to eat. I was doing a plate of cheese blintzes, and she—who knew?—some strawberry whole wheat pancakes.

She talked about punk rock as an instrument of liberation; *The Pedagogy of the Oppressed*; the commodification of revolution into t-shirts and cartoons; the grounds of real change. I'm originally a Village kid, so I was eating this all up along with a side order of potato *kluski*, but I was surprised to be hearing this from a bleached blonde from 'Bama, or wherever she was really from.

She talked more about her fractured family. I recall a string of houses, other people's kids as her "new brothers and sisters," with her ending up in a trailer park before she headed out for some school she called "State," although she never did say which one. She talked of classes in sociology and philosophy. I didn't hear anything about graduation. I heard a lot about her music, her art, and her wanting to "make a statement." I told her that if her gig the night before was any indication, the statements she'd be making would rank up there with the opening of the Seven Seals. That stunned her wordless. Then she leaned across the table and gave me a full-on kiss right there in the Kiev to a few tables of light applause.

The Awful Wrath started playing more and more dates. At CBGB, the band started off playing sets early in the evening, and over the course of a few months they slowly crept into the later (drunker, higher, and more prestigious) time slots. They also started to get press in the music pages. Music journalism on the Village beat came mostly in two flavors (then as now), cultist-like adulation and wiseass hatchets from hell. Among critics, the band developed a cult that worshipped, not just in The Awful Wrath's grotto, but at the altar of their lead singer, the writers using terms usually reserved for apocalyptic vision. "She is the beginning and the end, the Alpha and Omega," started one review in *Alphabet City Weekly*. The critic at the *Village Scream* wrote one week:

> Some bands want you to sell your soul to rock and roll. Others grab you by the throat and demand that you pay for your sins with blood: that is The Awful Wrath. Their high priestess waits for you at the altar, her knife raised high against a sky filled with the smoke of sacrifice.

Offstage, she was puzzled by this sort of language. She did not understand why all this religious and ritual imagery kept showing up in the reviews. The Awful Wrath had no stage act, no special costumes, no ritual bitings-off of rats' heads. This was a band; they played music, she sang the songs. We took our egg creams from Gem Spa and walked over to a late breakfast at Veselka, she and I kicking around our takes on the psyche of the music critic.

"What I think it comes down to is this," I said. "They feel something from you that they don't know what to do with. You put something out there that they've never really seen before. For them, it's beyond merely human; it's like something from a dark divinity. So they write about it in terms of a grim theology: blood sacrifices to a dark goddess. I think the real question is this: Where does this come from in *you?*"

We talked about the pain of her upbringing in a dozen bitter towns in the South. We talked about her rapes by 'cousins' and 'uncles,' from ages eight to sixteen. We also talked about how she had always brought a power to captivate to anything she did. She scared the living daylights out of the other kids when her Language Arts teachers led her fifth-grade class in a production of *Snow White*, with her playing the evil Queen. She was denied the female lead in *The Boyfriend* in tenth grade because her audition was "too adult," but her twelfth-grade performance as Helen Keller in *The Miracle Worker* increased donations to the local charities for the blind by fifty percent, for a year. She was an emotional maestro, with a talent for conveying and evoking emotions that few people could bring to any stage.

"What I want to do is rip the whole damn thing down," she said, after the wait staff at Veselka took our order.

"Which 'damn thing'?" I asked.

"The system. The rules that say it's okay to rape little girls, live like we were still the Confederacy, take the money from farmers out in the sticks and put it in the pockets of the bankers in town. Rip down the system that keeps kids stupid and sick if you're poor. Rip the whole thing down and burn it to ashes."

"Then what do you put *up?*"

"Damn," she said with a smile, "but you want me to think of *everything*, don't you?"

◆   ◆   ◆

The attention that The Awful Wrath got at gigs attracted a manager to them, a decent guy who kept them booked and got them paid on time. The band signed with a small indie label and started production on their first collection. I heard a lot of these cuts in the studio; they were harsh, brilliant send-ups of life in America, from the farms to the ghettos to the mansions and everything between. As their reputation grew, The Awful Wrath got invited to other, more-established band's gigs, as well as to their after-parties.

She and I and her bandmates were visiting a party in a suite of rooms at an old hotel in the West Twenties. Two bands staying on the same floor had decided to put on a big blast to celebrate the end of their respective gigs at different clubs. The party was loud, of course, and entertained a rough crowd—lines on the coffee table, needles on the bathroom sink—but that was fairly normal for the scene; she found out early on that few of her colleagues shared her taste for Paolo Freire or Frantz Fanon. We did not partake; me, because poli sci doctoral students can't afford to get wasted too often, and she, perhaps, to keep me company in my abstinence.

There is a point at every raucous party when it simply slows down, the flame burnt out; that's when people start to leave. At parties like this, though, many of the revelers are too exhausted to leave. People did not calm down so much as they collapsed, some into a state resembling coma, others into a languid torpor, from which they engaged other flagging souls in disjointed conversation.

"You know, baby," said one of the male members of the other bands to her, "you are really the top." He was sitting on the floor, propped up against a couch, cradling in his lap the head of one of the women laying on the floor. From this vantage point, that woman opened and closed her eyes as she slipped between worlds. "When you sing," the band member continued, "the crowd latches onto you like you are giving them the Word of God."

"Yeah," the woman in his lap said. "And I really gotta tell ya, I just hate your bloody guts." The man cradling her head started snickering.

"How come?" my singer said.

"Because you are just such a damn *goody*," said Lap Woman. "You grab the crowd and yank them the way no one else can. And you want them to *do* something. You want them to fix the world. We just want to drive them crazy."

"Yeah," the man cradling her head said, now giggling, "knife 'em and leave 'em to bleed in the aisles."

"You said it, *baby*," said Lap Woman. She turned her head towards his crotch and bit down hard into his parts. He howled, and she just bit in harder. He cursed and tried to push her head away, but he seemed to realize in the midst of this effort that this would separate him from his jewelry. He finally caught her in between clenches of her teeth, and shoved her head away. Other members of his band held her shoulders down to the cheap carpet while she laughed until she passed out. I called an ambulance and we left once the medics came.

Not long after that party, following a gig, I noticed that she was withdrawn, not wanting to say much. We were at the Kiev again, with the late crowd, and I asked her what was wrong.

"I'm wondering what good this all is," she said. "Everybody says I've got a special hold on the crowd, and maybe I do—but what good is it?"

At the next table over, two people who'd been at somebody's theatre afterparty were talking about Mozart. The guy sounded like a music history major—the Kiev was on the borders of NYU's and Cooper Union's territory, with the New School not far away—and his date had her chin in her hands, her blue eyes just soaking him all in.

"There are many theories as to why Mozart died," this guy said. "There are those who think it was some kind of atypical organ failure. Some think it was an infection passing through the area. But it is still a mystery, why one of the most famous men in the society of his time succumbed to illness at such an early age." He leaned in towards her. "So that's why some people think he was *poisoned!*"

My singer continued. "I mean, what do I actually get *done?* People dance around and scream to my music, but then no one goes and does anything. This is not changing the world."

It being three in the morning, I reached for the nearest cliché. "There's only so much one person can do," I said.

"What a pile of crap!" she answered. "One person can invent something that changes the world. A doctor can create an operation or discover a medicine that saves thousands of lives. And who are you to say something like that anyway? You're a freaking political science student. Why the hell would you even want to do that if you didn't want to change the world? Or are you too busy writing your dissertation to look at how messed up the world you're in really is? And you of all people know lots of situations where one person has made a difference. One person can write a book that starts a revolution."

"I guess I just don't know of anyone who's sung a song that started a revolution," I said. It was one of those things that, once you say it, you know you should have just shut up. But I had said it.

She didn't have an answer for this. We finished our *pierogen* and went back to our building in silence, going to our separate apartments. She left early in the afternoon for a tour of dives in Jersey and Philly; I was off teaching undergrad Poli Sci 101 when she left. I didn't know where she could be reached, and she never called. She got back while I was at a conference in DC, and when I returned she had already cleared out her apartment. Her note said she was getting a place with "some people" in Brooklyn. And that was that.

About two years later I saw her in a show at Max's II, the summer before it closed. We hadn't talked since that night in the Kiev. She had a bunch of new songs, and had the same hold over the crowd, but it seemed to me that there was a difference in her attitude. To me it looked like she alternated between a frantic wish to get something through to the audience, and a resignation to the idea that she never would. At the end of her last set, someone in the audience shouted something at her like "we love you"; she answered with her last words over the mic, "Yeah. Thanks." I left without going backstage.

And now, years on, she's dead. They're talking about some kind of catastrophic reaction to a flu infection. There will be a tribute collection. Being the dinosaur that my snarky New School students say I am, I'll get it and refer to it as an "album."

I know how Mozart died. Sure, what the coroners call the proximate cause might have been an assassin's poison, or some funky organ failure, or a bug sweeping through Vienna or Prague. But that was just the final step, the burglar that crept through the open window and stole his life. But how did the window happen to be left open?

I think that at some point Mozart looked ahead and saw his likely futures. He was already the man that so many lesser composers wanted dead, and that would not change. The worst thing, though, was that he was, in his time, one of the very few people who "got" his music. He wrote about the virtues of the Enlightenment and Masonic wisdom in *The Magic Flute*, but hardly anyone thinks Mozart really *furthered* the Enlightenment. His patrons were largely philistines who went to the opera to make the scene, not revolution. A giant in a world of ants, Mozart must have been lonely beyond comprehension. No one can live like that for too long; one way or the other, some part of his soul would seek escape, and whether the means of his escape came in a poisoner's potion or an infection or some wasting syndrome, that part of him would accept his end, even embrace it.

As did she, I think. And as will I, some day.

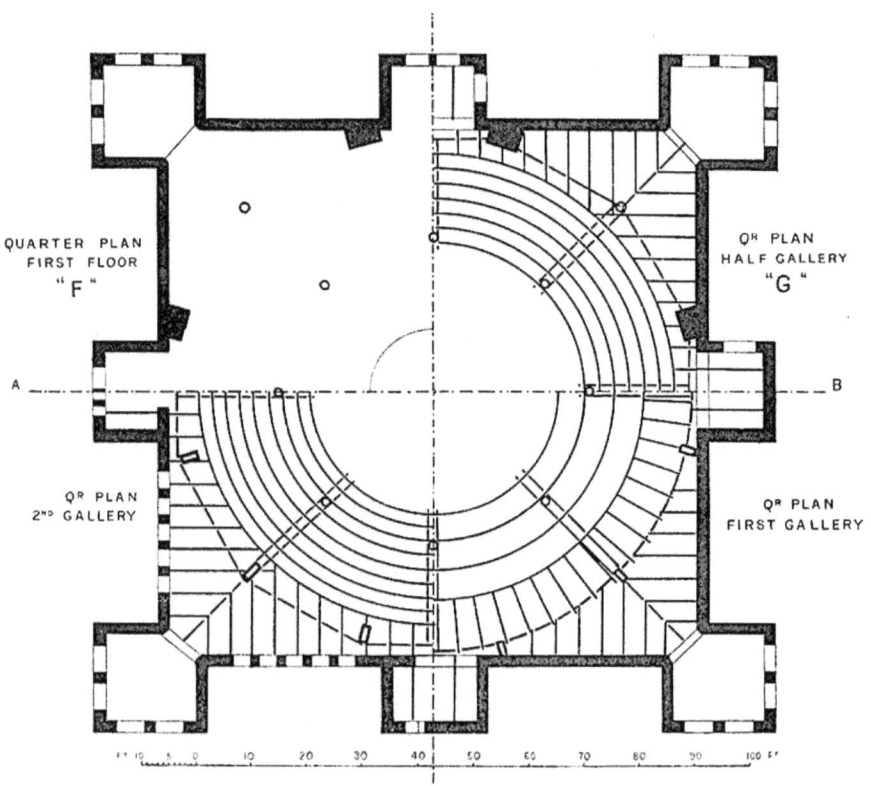

QUARTER PLAN
FIRST FLOOR
"F"

Qᴿ PLAN
HALF GALLERY
"G"

Qᴿ PLAN
2ᴺᴰ GALLERY

Qᴿ PLAN
FIRST GALLERY

A

B

FT 10   5   0   10   20   30   40   50   60   70   80   90   100 FT

The Blueprints

HE FOUND THE BLUEPRINTS about an hour before dawn, just outside the rear entrance to the Steinway Building. He was walking east along West Fifty-Eighth Street to get a couple of bagels at the 24-hour delicatessen near the corner of Sixth Avenue, when he passed a group of trash bins at the curb, one filled with rolls of blueprints. These had been discarded, the twenty-year-old imagined, by some architectural firm that occupied an office, either upstairs in the Steinway Building, or in the large old office building next door. After staring for a moment at the bin with the blueprints, he walked on to the deli, got his two bagels and orange juices, and ate one of the bagels on the corner of Sixth and Fifty-Eighth, looking at the pre-dawn September sky over Central Park, to the north. He slung the plastic bag with his remaining bagel and juice over his left wrist. Now that he did not need to keep his fingers clean, as he walked back west along Fifty-Eighth, he snagged a roll of blueprints at random from the bin.

He returned to his desk in the lobby of one of the large apartment buildings on West Fifty-Eighth between Sixth and Seventh Avenues, a block north of Carnegie Hall. This was, of course, one of the tonier neighborhoods in Manhattan, and many of the apartment buildings here merited a night staff. At the lobby, he relieved the night maintenance chief, who went back to whatever the night maintenance chief did down in the basement before dawn. The bagel-and-blueprints-laden lobby attendant washed his hands, ate his second bagel, and inspected the blueprints.

He had never looked closely at blueprints before, but he found the symbolic language of walls, doors, and windows easy to decipher. The sheaf of blueprints that he had grabbed proved to include plans for a miscellaneous variety of interior structures: offices, mostly, but also residences, corporate atria, even a contemporary worship space. Then he came upon the blueprints for a library.

It was hard to tell whether the plan was for some school or office space, but he decided, on the basis of little but his own desire, that this was probably the plan for a personal library, albeit on a grander scale than anything he had ever seen before. A "library" in the *New York Times*' real estate sections he'd seen usually meant a room of books with built-in bookcases—something he would have loved to have, but nothing to make the heart race. However, the library shown in the blueprints was a different creation altogether.

The planned library had two levels, a grand reading area the size of a small ballroom, and a wrap-around gallery above, which communicated with the area below by two winding staircases placed in diagonally opposite corners. The elevation renderings revealed that each level was twelve feet tall.

The gallery had floor-to-near-ceiling bookcases, each holding 18-inch-tall shelves, with sliding library ladders placed along a bar running along the top. The lower level featured similar bookcases along one wall, one of the long sides of a rectangle, while the other long wall had floor-to-ceiling windows, looking out on some vista one could only imagine. (He thought that such a magnificent library could only look out on Central Park.)

The lower level was entered through a double door in one of the short walls, flanked by two pillars labeled "J" PILLAR (*not "A"?*, he wondered) and "B" PILLAR. He did not have the renderings for the pillars in the materials he had pulled from the bin, and the rumble and crunch of the waste collection truck passing by a few minutes earlier told him that it was too late to go back to look for them now. However, the mere fact that the blueprints in his possession made reference to such renderings meant that even the entry pillars must have been no thoughtless decoration. The other, shorter wall of the rectangle was designated MURAL, and he could only wonder what it would have shown.

One corner of the lower level was designated MEDIA AREA, with spaces set aside for a microfilm/microfiche reader, a computer, and a printer, along with storage cabinets. (The single quantities of each machine bolstered his conviction that this was a personal library, although a lavish one.) A few tall stand-alone bookcases were on the lower level as well, with a huge globe situated in one corner, and a reading stand designated for an atlas. The center of the carpeted room held an ample reading table, with two lamps, a table stand for a dictionary, and six chairs. (*A family with children?*, he wondered.) The whole room was topped by a curved ceiling, a flattened dome, painted like a sky just at dawn or dusk, with clouds, and stars in recognizable constellations.

It was, in summary, a Temple of the Book. In his heart, he was already a priest there.

He put most of the blueprints into the paper recycling bin in the stairwell off the lobby. He carefully rolled up the blueprints describing the library, and put a couple of rubber bands around the roll. At seven o'clock in the morning his shift ended, and he took his treasure home on the subway, riding the F train under the skyscrapers of midtown, down and across Manhattan to the Lower East Side, and his rent-controlled apartment on East Second Street near First Avenue. It was the kind of neighborhood where appliance repair stores jostled hole-in-the-wall art galleries, and a bar's open-mic poetry reading's all-night afterparty could suddenly turn violent. When he got home, he re-rolled the blueprints, print side out, to begin the process of taking the curl out of them.

The previous month, he had picked up a set of "demotivational" posters in cheap but large metal frames, discarded during some company's relocation from Fifty-Seventh Street. (One advantage of working the night shift in midtown was that it put him in position for premium finds on trash collection nights.) One poster, for example, showed a partially constructed highway cloverleaf, with part of the road terminating in midair. The caption read: "Going Nowhere? Embrace your destiny." He did not care for the posters much himself; he had brought them home because it reminded him of the kind of dead-end humor that his father would have appreciated, although his father had died almost a year before. He stripped the posters of their frames, put the naked posters out on Second Street for someone else to claim, and used the frames for his blueprints of the library: the lower floor from above, the gallery from above, two side elevations of the whole, and the ceiling from below, showing small recessed lighting fixtures positioned as stars in the twilight sky. He still could not decide whether the scene was of dusk or dawn.

At first glance, his apartment was not a likely place for a set of library blueprints. Any sort of literature was very little in evidence: a couple of sports almanacs, some issues of *TV Guide* that had piled up. He still kept his own small stash of books in a tiny bookcase hidden behind his clothes in the bedroom closet.

His father had not approved of his interest in books, or of education generally. Instead, his father had placed a great deal of emphasis on practical knowledge: how to fix a leaky boiler, how to test for dry rot hiding under a painted wooden surface, how to handicap a horserace or figure the point spread in the Super Bowl. In vain had the young man tried to explain to his father how one might find practical implications for the present in the study of the past, say, or even—heaven forbid—in literature. His father would have none of it.

When he was near the conclusion of elementary school, he had been offered a choice opportunity. The school principal nominated him to be one of two graduating eighth-grade boys from this elementary school to take the entrance examination to a high school directed by Jesuits on the Upper East Side, where all students received a full scholarship for a rigorous college preparatory education. It would have been his ticket to a place where the life of the mind was appreciated, but his father was strictly opposed. "I won't have your head filled up with useless things," his father had said; later that night, his father had explained why poker players should never draw to an inside straight. If his mother were alive, he had thought, she would have let him take that examination, but his mother had died the summer after his sixth grade. Another boy was chosen to take the examination in his place; last he heard, that boy was now in his junior year at Yale.

On the wall behind the television hung icons of his father's personal religion: commemorative sports jerseys celebrating championship victories of the Yankees, the Knicks, the Nets, the Mets, the Rangers, and the Giants. He sat on the couch looking at those posters, remembering the games he had attended with his father a couple of times a year for over a decade; he would cheer for whichever team his father cheered for, not because he really cared who won, but because it gave him the opportunity to agree with his father about something. He remembered how he would feign tiredness and go off to his room, ostensibly for a nap, to sneak some reading while his father watched games on television, throughout the weekend. He thought about his father in this vein for some time, looking at the relics of his father's faith.

He took down each of the sports jerseys, put them away in his father's dresser, and hung the blueprints of the library in their stead. He moved his small bookcase out of his bedroom closet into the living room. Then he telephoned the daytime maintenance supervisor at his Fifty-Eight Street building and asked him to set aside some scrap wood boards that he had seen in the basement; he had more shelving to build. By one in the afternoon, he was in bed. His last thought before sleep was the decision that the ceiling artwork in the blueprints were a depiction of the sky just before dawn.

Over the next few weeks, he changed a lot about his apartment on Second Street. He used his father's tools to build two bookcases, each with five wide and tall shelves, and he placed these prominently in the living room. He visited East Village Books, Alabaster Books, the Strand, and the discount table at St. Marks Books, and began to accumulate a larger personal library, featuring literature, current events, and especially history. A year after his father's death, he threw out all his father's ashtrays, and went through his father's belongings, preserving some items as keepsakes, and donating the rest to the Salvation Army.

During those weeks of renovation, he spent a little time every day looking at the blueprints. At the end of a month, in the fading light of an early evening in October, he stood leaning on the living room window sill of his fifth floor walk-up. He looked out north onto Second Street, onto the East Village beyond, and, far away, he saw the towers of midtown, crowned by the Empire State Building and his personal favorite among New York skyscrapers, the Chrysler Building, the closest thing to the Emerald City of Oz that he had ever seen in real life. He decided that he wanted the library in the blueprints, the library and everything that it represented: knowledge, refinement, that family with children, financial success. He had been a good son to his father, but his father was gone, the depth of his mourning was past, and now he had his own journey to plot out.

He enrolled in classes at Manhattan Community College in the spring. The modest inheritance that he had received from his father's life insurance policies permitted him to cut back his hours on West Fifty-Eighth Street. He took out student loans to transfer to City College as a full-time undergraduate, majoring in history. Because no one told him that undergraduates were incapable of doing serious historical work, he published three scholarly papers on New York City history by the time he graduated, including his senior thesis on the history of the New York Public Library. These earned him a spot in the doctoral history program at Columbia.

His doctoral studies broadened his world beyond Manhattan. He spent a year in England and France studying the origins of the European Enlightenment. He presented scholarly papers at conferences in Chicago, San Francisco, and London (where the obliquely intersecting streets reminded him of the West Village). At one of these meetings, he met an American studies graduate student from Yale, and she cheered him enthusiastically at his Columbia doctoral hooding ceremony, the week before they were married. That fall, he took a position on the history faculty of NYU.

That same year, in addition to more scholarly work, he published the first of what became a series of books on the lessons of history, written for a popular audience. Critics attributed the unexpected success of this series to "the common touch" that he had, in bringing out the implications of the politics of the eighteenth century English Enlightenment, say, for the education of high-schoolers in twenty-first century America. The public television series that followed got him labeled as "the Carl Sagan of popular history." Then there were the historical novels he wrote, followed by the movies based on them.

Six years after the completion of his doctorate, he and his wife (now a professor at Columbia) bought a distressed brownstone under repossession in the East Seventies. A year of renovation (and their second child) later, he had his two-level library.

There were differences, of course. The doors opened up on one of the long walls, not the short ones, as the blueprints had indicated. The tall bay window looked out onto a school playground rather than Central Park; there was only one winding staircase between the levels; and, the ceiling had only painted stars, not light fixtures; the room had pocket doors opening on the dining room opposite the bay window, not a mural. Yet, for all that, his library was the embodiment of the plans laid out in the blueprints that he had plucked from the trash years before, blueprints that now, in nicer frames, hung on the walls of the library itself.

The couple held a housewarming party for some new neighbors and colleagues soon after the renovations were finished. He noticed one woman, a neighbor, inspecting the framed blueprints in the library with particular intensity. He approached the guest, explained the provenance of the blueprints, and asked her what she found so interesting.

"I know these plans," the guest said.

"How so?"

"A firm I worked for, years ago, put these together. The client was some banker who wound up losing a lot of his money in Madoff's Ponzi scheme. He moved to Florida and remade himself as some kind of novelist, I think. My firm went broke not long afterwards, in the Great Recession. They would have tossed these plans then."

"So the library was never built?"

"Nope," the guest said. "Never built." She looked around the room. "Not until now, anyway."

After the party was over and the children—one each named for his wife's mother and his own father—were put to bed, he went out onto the rooftop terrace and looked south onto the towers of midtown, the Chrysler Building sparkling in the distance. He thought of the blueprints, the library never built, and the library newly born. He thought of the course of his own life, and how much of its reinvention had been catalyzed by the scraps of someone else's discarded plans, made into a symbol of his own aspirations. That got him thinking about the role of personal aspirations in changing societies throughout history. He went downstairs to the library to make some notes about these ideas, before going up to his wife and their bed.

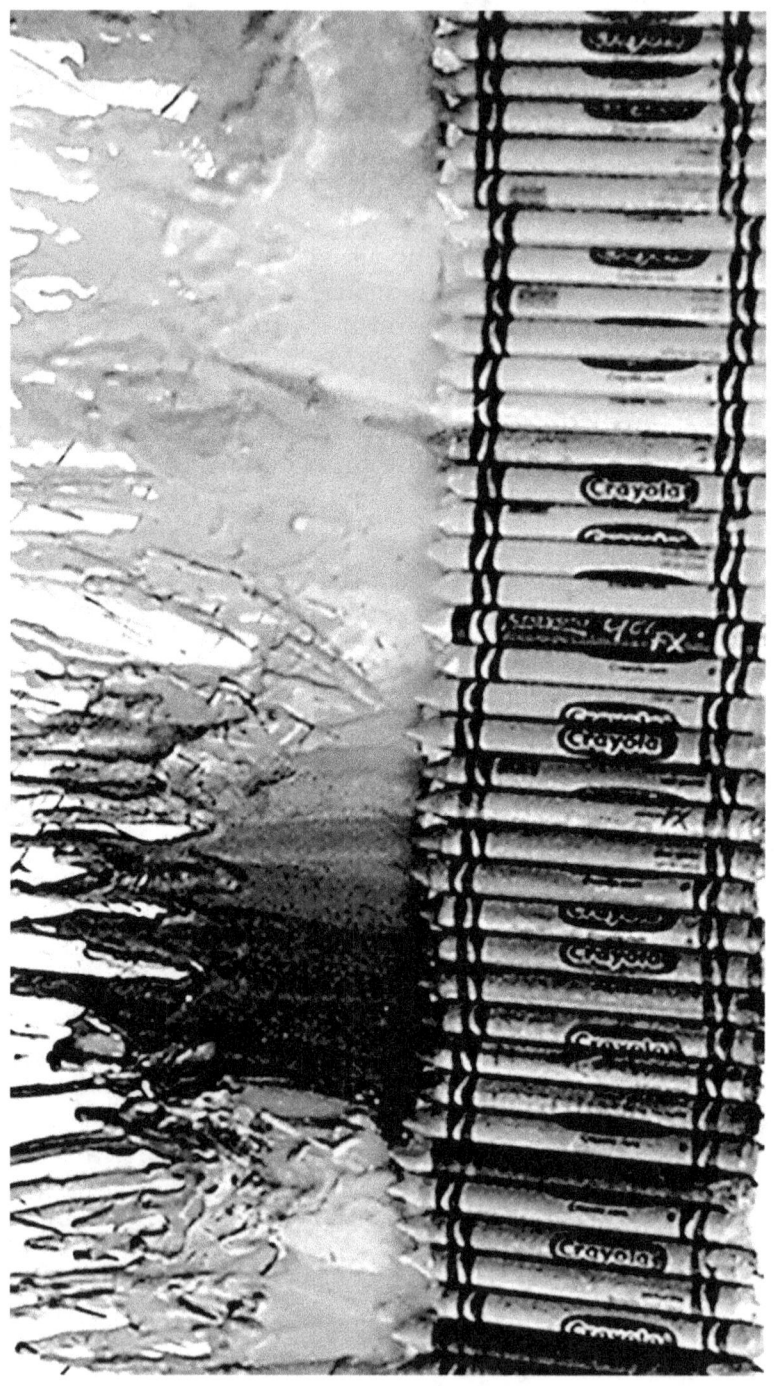

The Lines

YOUR FATHER IS VISITING, as he does occasionally now that you are five, and your mother is yelling at him for his long absence. She throws a coloring book with a small box of crayons at the couch where he sits. "Here! *Do* something with your son, why don't you." He sits you up next to him on the couch and turns to a page of the coloring book, a line drawing of a big duck in a sailor suit next to a surprised-looking horse wearing a straw hat, thick black lines on cheap white paper. He puts a crayon in your hands and guides you in filling a space, saying, "The most important thing is to color inside the lines."

A couple of years later, you are sitting on the floor of that same living room. Your mother has a broom in a two-fisted grip, making a line of force pushing your father, a much larger man, out of your apartment. You see that he isn't putting up much of a struggle. He is talking funny and moving strangely. Your mother pushes him, and he stays outside the boundary set by the broom; he steps outside the apartment and never returns.

Many years later, you realize that he was high that day.

Sister Nina in the fourth grade is telling the class that the moon doesn't rotate, that's why we see just one side of it all the time. You have read every astronomy book in the school library twice, and you speak up to say no, the moon's period of rotation on its axis is the same as its period of revolution around the earth, and that's why we only see the one side of the moon. It's about lines of force, gravity and axes. You are right, and you are smacked for overstepping the boundary between teacher and student.

You keep correcting your teachers. You keep getting punished.

A couple of years later, civics class at St. Stanislaus School is all about that year's March on Washington, and Sister Janice is talking about ethnic groups like they are shoeboxes people neatly fit into, the Polish are like *this* and the Blacks are like *thus* and the Puerto Ricans are like *that*, and you ask, but what if you're Polish *and* Puerto Rican *and* Black, and even the kids whispering dirty jokes in the corner become totally silent, and Sister Janice changes the lesson to silent reading time, followed by singing. La-la-la-la-la-la-*la*.

The white kids beat you up for being Puerto Rican. The Puerto Rican kids beat you up for being white. The Black guys beat you up for what little money you have. *I am an Equal Opportunity whup-ass magnet*, you think. Over the course of many years you develop your own style of self-defense, a combination of karate taught to you by an Okinawan in Japan, and Lower East Side street fighting of the dirtiest sort. Strange as it seems to you, just when you become most capable of dealing with threat, people stop bothering you.

In college you join a church that isn't Catholic or Protestant or Orthodox, and you like that it doesn't fit in with the others.

You work at an international Madison Avenue firm to support your family while you go to grad school nights and weekends. You teach spreadsheet software to advertising executives in the first wave of people learning to use computers at their desks. Some new account executive insists on telling you a story about his car suddenly disintegrating, and you say it ended just like "The Wonderful One-Hoss Shay." He looks at you as if you were some odd chimera and asks, "What is a computer guy doing reading poetry?"

In grad school you bring in topics that few people in the psychology department want to talk about: transcendent experiences, meditation, religion, personal worldviews. But the faculty are so divided among themselves ideologically that there is no party line to enforce. You are very happy.

*   *   *

Your father's sons by other women, not his wives, call to say that your long-gone father is dead. How did they find you? you wonder aloud. "He had a line for you in his address book," quite a current listing, even though he disappeared decades ago. The casket is closed because, they say, the zig-zag scars from that brain surgery at the end are just too awful to look at. You learn that, while you had been teaching religion in Asia years before, he had been serving, too—a sentence of twenty-five-to-life in a federal maximum-security prison. "Your father was guilty of having the wrong friends, friends on the wrong side of the line from the law," your uncle says. Better lawyers got your father out in a year or two, and he went back to snorting line upon line after line.

You intern at a hospital and the benefits staff is taking down information for your insurance coverage and their demographic survey. "What is your heritage?" she asks. You explain that you are multi-ethnic, Puerto Rican and Polish and Eastern European Jew, and probably Black, and she says "Pick *one*," holding up her index finger like Sisters Nina and Janice used to do. You refuse to pick one, because you really *do* embrace multitudes.

You remarry, this time to a Cherokee-Northwestern European mixed-race woman. You figure that between the two of you, your ancestral lines have most of Europe and the Americas covered at the very least, peddlers and peasants, Cherokee and Taino Nations, *conquistadores*, Vikings, *conversos, marranos y moriscos*, yeomen "and yeowomen" (she says), potato farmers, Visigoths, Ostrogoths, Vandals, and Moors, and, as far as you can tell, Afro-Caribbean slaves, chiefs and *caciques*, rabbis and *rebbes* and shamans and *santeros y santeras* and chest-ripping Aztec priests, so people should *not* mess with you and yours or half the conquerors and conquered of Western Civilization with all their demons and angels, gods and goddesses would chase them into the wine-dark sea.

You win a national award in academic psychology. At the convention, the awards presenter introduces you as an excellent example of "hybrid vigor." You think, *you don't know the half of it, baby.*

Your psychology friends don't get that your writing thing is not a "hobby." Your writing friends are confused by your doing psychology stuff. Nobody pronounces your hyphenated name correctly, although they differ on which part they screw up. You just go on doing what you do and being who you are.

You are remembering what it was like to teach your kids to color when they were little. You sat them down next to you on the couch, with a big box of crayons. You put a blank pad of paper in front of them and asked, "what do you want to draw today?"

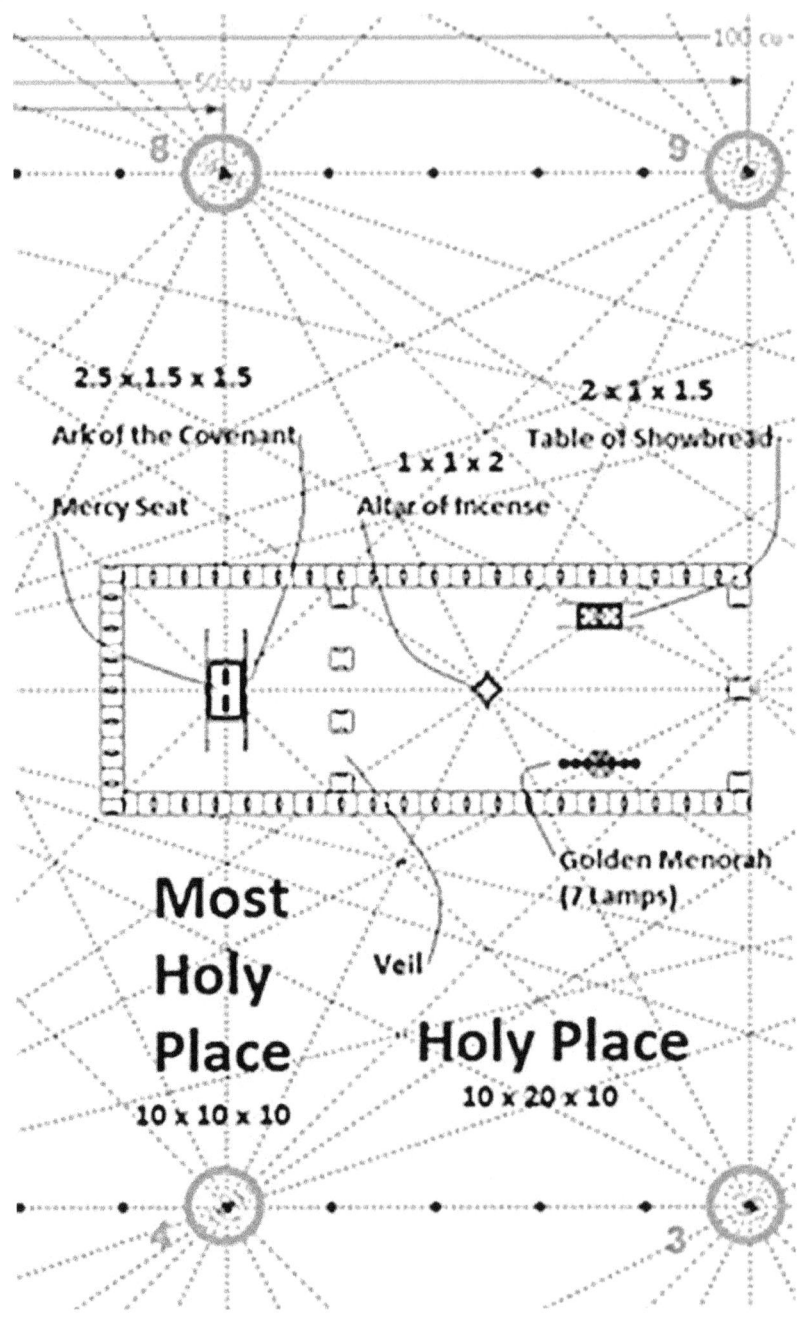

2.5 x 1.5 x 1.5

Ark of the Covenant

Mercy Seat

1 x 1 x 2

Altar of Incense

2 x 1 x 1.5

Table of Showbread

Golden Menorah
(7 Lamps)

**Most
Holy
Place**

10 x 10 x 10

Veil

Holy Place

10 x 20 x 10

The Most Holy Place

ON A BRIGHT DAY in late June, after breakfast and his medication for diabetes, Michael Kozak began to shred his unopened Christmas cards.

Michael started by doing some rough sorting. Cards from his three older sisters and his older brother went right into Michael's industrial-strength paper shredder, first off. He did not want to see the annual photocopied letters, the pictures of their children and grandchildren. Then the cards from their children's families went into the shredder. *Family comes first*, he thought.

He saved the cards from his own three children and their families for the end of the family pile. He paused for a few moments with the envelopes in his hand, thick envelopes that promised to hold personal messages from his kids and drawings from his grandchildren. He wanted to open these very badly. But the years of his hurt had been a few too many. Ultimately these cards also went into the shredder, followed by cards from many others who were not family.

It was a bit late in the year for Michael to shred his cards. His preference was to shred everything by the time of the Martin Luther King holiday, allowing him to include not only his November birthday cards and the Christmas (and, curiously, Hanukkah) cards, but the cards celebrating the Winter Solstice, New Year's, and Three Kings, which people still kept sending to him, despite the fact that he had not sent out cards of any sort for the last quarter of a century. However, increasingly over the last year or so, Michael found himself feeling out of sorts, and so he got behind on his mail, and was more inclined to let things fall between the cracks. Many of the tenants in his rental houses and apartments in Poughkeepsie had moved out, and some had died, but he had not cleared out most of the houses or apartments that had become vacant in almost a year.

Yet, when June twenty-fifth came around, Michael decided that his procrastination had gone too far. *Once you reach*

71

the opposite end of the year from Christmas, the cards have to go, he thought. But he would never just put personal information into the trash, hence the shredder.

Having finished off his Christmas cards, Michael looked at his "Look At Later" letter tray, which held two stacks of mail, in unkempt piles, each at least two feet tall, *I could just shred it all*, he thought, *start off clean.* But he knew that would be irresponsible, and so he swore to himself to work on those piles for fifteen minutes a day. *Starting tomorrow.*

As he sat contemplating his "Look At Later" tray, a lofty tower which commanded a view of the riotous landscape of paper that constituted the top of his desk, he heard through the open window of his home office the sound of a car approaching, then parking in his driveway. Michael got up from his chair and snuck over to the side of his office's second-story window, looking through the flimsy curtain at the car that had just arrived. The car doors opened, and two men in their later sixties stepped out, crunching the gravel on Michael's driveway.

Oh, that one, Michael thought, recognizing the older of the two men. The duo walked up to Michael's front door, leaving the range of his sight; Michael heard the doorbell ring. A little while later, it rang again; then, still later, a third time. *Persistent, you've got to give them that*, Michael thought. The two men spoke for a moment to each other, but Michael could not make out their words. The two reentered the car and drove off, as Michael took care to conceal himself around the edge of the window frame.

Michael took the most recent three-ring binder of *The Book of Michael* off the shelf next to his desk. He thought about writing an entry about the annoyance of unwanted visitors, but he decided against it; the two-inch binder of Volume 5 was already overstuffed with loose leaf paper; he really needed to start off Volume 6, and that required a trip to the office supply store for another binder. He had addressed the topic before, several times, so there was no urgent need to address it again.

Yet, pulling Volume 5 off the shelf got him to looking over the whole of *The Book of Michael*, which put him into a reverie about how badly he had been treated by the world and so many of the people within it. For *The Book of Michael* was a chronicle of grievances, beginning with his divorce thirty-five years earlier. And what a chronicle it was, darting here to years predating his divorce, as he cursed his parents for *their* split-up; darting there to whatever day he was writing on, for sufficient to each day was the evil thereof; then, back to his wife, who, in the days before he had the money it would have taken to get a lawyer to stop her, took their three kids off to Boston, over three hundred miles from the home they had shared in Poughkeepsie, where he had remained; then back to the academic advisor who had forced him out of his abortive graduate program at SUNY-Purchase; and so on, and so forth, through over two thousand loose leaf sheets of loss and damage.

Michael just looked over some highlights. Two hours later, he was ready for lunch and went downstairs.

Passing through the living room on his way to the kitchen, Michael noticed that an envelope had been slipped under his front door, no doubt by his two unwanted visitors. He found that they must have typed it in advance, expecting not to actually meet him.

> Dear Brother Kozak,
>
> We hope that all is well with you on this lovely day. I (Dan) have missed meeting with you over the last few months, and I (Luis) look forward to getting to know you. My (Dan's) wife Jan told me that she saw you at the Greenmarket last week and that you looked well, so we're happy for that.
>
> At church, the ward is doing well. The oldest Petersen boy left for his mission to Hiroshima last week, and the Takamiyagis had their babies (twins!). There will be a lot of fun things this summer, a 4th of July picnic and a handcart reenactment on Pioneer Day, and we hope you can enjoy these too.
>
> We'll be calling soon to make an appointment to see you, and we hope that we can arrange that soon. In the meantime, please don't hesitate to contact us if there is anything at all that we can do for you.

Best regards,
Dan Kimball   tel. ###-###-###
Luis Echevarria tel. ###-###-###

So the local Mormon congregation was still reaching out to Michael with lay pastoral visitors. *Damn*, he thought, *don't they have lazy 'home teachers' anymore?* He only went to church when his kids visited, and no one was scheduled to come by any time soon. The handcart pioneer reenactment would have to go on without him.

The phone rang, and Michael's answering machine went straight to message-screening mode.

"Dad, it's Tom. Please pick up. Please, it's really important. Pick up, Dad."

Michael stuffed his home teachers' letter into his pocket and picked up the call. "Yes, Tommy, Dad here. What's up?"

"It's Millie."

Millicent Kozak was the eleven-year-old daughter of Tom and his wife Penelope. Early that morning, when Tom and Penelope went to rouse their four kids for school, Millie would not wake up, although she was breathing. Millie was now in the emergency room with her parents, and was soon to be moved to the intensive care unit. "I thought you'd want to know," Tom said.

Tom and his family lived in Kingston, less than half an hour by car farther north along the Hudson River from Michael's house in Poughkeepsie. Michael made it to the hospital quickly. After some of the tests came back, Michael, Tom, and Penelope met with Millie's doctor at Star of Bethlehem Hospital.

"We've done a spinal tap on Millie," Dr. Corman said, "and now we know for sure that she has bacterial meningitis. And there we have some good news and some bad news."

"Start with the bad news," Penelope said.

"Actually, I need to start the other way around," Corman said. "The good news is that the bacterial form of meningitis is the kind that we can usually treat with an intensive course of antibiotics." Penelope's eyebrows redeployed from 'frantically anxious' mode to just 'highly concerned.'

Dr. Corman continued. "The bad news is that there are some hints that this is an unusual form of bacterial meningitis. We won't know until—"

"But how is it unusual?" Tom asked. "I mean, like, what's usual and what's unusual here?" His eyebrows had been at the 'frantic' setting since before he got to the hospital.

Dr. Corman paused for a moment after Tom's interruption was finished. "As I was saying, we won't know for sure until the tests come back, and we'll know then whether there's really cause for concern."

Michael smiled and politely raised an index finger to gain Dr. Corman's attention. When Dr. Corman turned to Michael, the latter's smile disappeared as he asked, "Concern. About. *What?*"

Dr. Corman paused another moment. "It is possible that this is an antibiotic-resistant form of bacterial meningitis."

Michael asked, "And what would be the likely prognosis if this *is* the treatment-resistant form?"

Dr. Corman paused for two beats. "Not good."

Penelope's and Thomas's brows furrowed as they looked to the floor, their eyebrows now at 'catastrophe' setting.

"So when will those tests be in? Michael asked.

"Another hour so or," Dr. Corman said.

Michael, Penelope, and Tom sat in a waiting area just outside the ICU. The waiting area was decorated in pastel colors and muted-earth-toned furniture that looked to Michael just like the color of the muddy feces of a very sick dog.

Penelope said, "I just wish we could get in to see her and give her a blessing,"

"Honey," said Tom, "I will do that just as soon as they let us in." His blank gaze was fixed on a tuft of caca-colored carpeting two feet in front of where he sat.

"But it's better if two priesthood holders give the blessing," Penelope said. She looked at Michael. "Everyone we know at our ward is away on vacation," she explained. Tom and Penelope attended a Mormon congregation composed largely of young married couples with small children; once school was out, most families took off for vacation through Independence Day. "Michael," she asked, "would you even consider ...?"

It had been several national Presidents ago since Michael had participated in giving a priesthood blessing. When Michael and his wife split up, he left behind any real activity in their shared religion. His grudge was with her, but he took it out on God, for reasons so vague that even he could not have articulated them.

Michael got up from his chair to get away from Penelope's pleading look, and walked over to a window, putting his hands in his pockets. There his left hand came upon a piece of paper that Michael pulled out: his home teachers' note. In contrast to Tom and Penelope's ward, Michael's was full of older couples. Dan Kimball was retired, and was certainly still in town.

"Tell you what, Penny," Michael said, still looking at Dan's telephone number, "I've got an even better idea."

Forty minutes later, Dan Kimball, Michael, and Tom were all wearing hospital gowns, face masks, booties, and latex gloves in the isolation room of the ICU. The young nurse in charge of the area at this hour did not want to let in more than two visitors at a time, but Michael was good with a glare, and told a story that made three people seem necessary for a two-person ritual. Luis sat out in the waiting area keeping company with Penelope. Before the three gowned visitors lay Millie, her breathing barely detectable, pale as ever Michael had seen her.

"Brethren, as I understand it, the laying on of hands requires actual *hands*," Dan said, as he started to take off his rubber gloves. "But that's my take on it, and neither of you should feel obligated to do the same." Tom started taking his gloves off.

"In for a dime, in for a dollar," Michael said, as he started taking off his gloves, too.

Dan positioned himself near the head of the bed on Millie's right, next to the IV drip, with Tom on her left. Michael stood next to his son. *Poor kid looks like he might just fall over*, Michael thought. *I'd better be here to catch him.*

Before putting on his gown, Tom had removed a tiny cylindrical metal vial from his key ring. Now, at Millie's bedside, Tom produced the vial, unscrewed the top, gave the top to his father, and positioned the open vial just above the top of Millie's forehead. He held the vial there until two drops of olive oil fell upon Millie's head just below her hairline. Tom handed the vial to Michael, and placed his hands gently upon Millie's forehead, over the oil.

"Millicent Arwen Kozak," Tom said, "by the power and authority of the holy Melchizedek priesthood, which I bear, I anoint you with this oil, which has been consecrated for the healing of the sick. This I do in the name of Jesus Christ, Amen."

Michael and Dan added their own "Amen" in unison. Tom lifted his hands from Millie's head; he screwed the top of the vial back on and stowed it in a pocket.

Dan placed his two hands lightly on Millie's head where Tom's hands had been. Tom placed his hands above Dan's, and placed them so that his fingertips touched Millie's head. Michael did the same.

"Millicent Arwen Kozak," Dan said, "by the power and authority of the holy Melchizedek priesthood, which we bear, we lay our hands upon you and seal this anointing that you have received, and I pronounce unto you this blessing by the power of the Holy Spirit."

Tom had asked Dan to do the sealing because Tom was too upset to think straight, and because Tom knew better than to ask his father. Michael had refused all such requests since Michael's now-ex had moved away with their kids.

Dan paused before saying the words of blessing, a part of the ritual that was not scripted, and was supposed to be spoken as the Spirit dictated. The pause, a common practice, did not bother Michael at first. But then the usual three seconds or so of silence stretched to thirty, before Dan spoke.

"Sister Millie," Dan said, "your Father in Heaven is well-pleased with you for the progress you have made in your life on earth. He is well-pleased with the charity and Christlike love you have shown to others...."

As Dan continued in this vein, Michael was not sure he liked the direction in which this blessing was heading. Usually, this would have been the point where the person pronouncing the blessing rebuked the illness, or commanded the sick to be made whole. What Dan was saying sounded like something else altogether: a eulogy.

Dan continued. "We bless you to proceed along the path that God has put you on, until finally you come into the presence of your Heavenly Parents again. This I pronounce upon you in the name of Jesus Christ, Amen."

Tom added his "Amen" immediately; Michael stared at Dan for a moment and then said "Amen." The three of them took their hands from Millie's head.

Tom bent over and kissed Millie where the oil had left a tiny damp spot on her forehead. "I'm going to sit here with Millie awhile," he said. "You can let Penelope in."

In the ICU staff washroom, first Michael and then Dan changed back into their street clothes, discarding the gloves and masks, and putting the gowns and booties into hampers. When Dan finished, he made to go out to the waiting area, but Michael spoke and stopped him.

"What the hell kind of blessing was *that?*" Michael asked. "No healing, no rebuking, no commanding, no *nothing.* What's that supposed to do for her? What's that going to do to Tommy and Penny?"

Dan turned to Michael, looking ten years older than he had when he arrived at the hospital. "Believe me, I understand," Dan said. "I've never given a blessing like that before. It's not what I thought I'd be saying. But it's what the Spirit told me." They looked at each other in silence. "Look," Dan continued, "it didn't *say* that she'll—"

"Enough!" Michael said. "Let's let Penny visit now."

As they walked into the waiting area, they found Dr. Corman telling Penelope and Luis that Millie had the antibiotic-resistant form of the bacterial infection in the tissues that enveloped her brain and spine. Penelope started to cry; Michael held her, and Dan left to suit up again and go into the isolation room to get Tom.

The nursing shift changed at 4 p.m. The head night nurse assured Tom, Penelope, and Michael that, given the counter-measures that the medical staff was taking, and Millie's current stable condition, it was very unlikely that there would be any crisis that night. In any event, the hospital would contact Millie's parents immediately upon any change in her condition. The nurse advised them all to get some sleep at home, at least tonight. Michael backed the nurse up, and saw to it that Tom and Penelope set off for home.

Michael picked up a sandwich at a drive-through on the way home, parked in his driveway, and carried the crumply paper bag as he trudged along the crunchy gravel to his door. After he ate, he sat and stared at the day's light turn from late afternoon to early evening, outside his living room window. He thought about Millie and her brief life to date. *Such a sweet child*, he thought. She had sent him homemade birthday and Christmas cards; he had seen them in the pile that he had shredded just that morning, a morning that now seemed a very long time in the past.

Michael remembered that a couple of years before, when he was still opening presents instead of discarding them, Millie had made a Christmas tree ornament for him. He wanted to see that ornament now.

Upstairs, Michael entered the room where he stored his long-unused Christmas decorations, the bedroom of his late father, Maciek. Michael pulled up the shades of his father's windows for light, and dug through what had been his father's closet and found the right box of tree ornaments, as the sun began to set in the bedroom window.

Millie's tree ornament was an awkward little thing, really a styrofoam ball a bit smaller than a fist, covered in cheap gold glitter, with small photos of Millie pinned into place around the outside, like a little Globe of Millie's World: Millie as a baby playing with the blocks that Maciek and Michael had gotten her; Millie dressed and made up like a little mouse for Halloween; eight-year-old Millie dressed for her baptism in white. White like a shroud. Something broke in Michael, and he wept and wept.

The last rays of the sun had crept far up Maciek's wall of photographs, when Michael finished crying. They only still shone on the topmost item, not a photo but an illustration.

It was the framed handout from a presentation that Maciek had delivered before a group of Freemasons, many years before, "The Symbolism of the Temple Built by Solomon and the Tabernacle Built by Moses." Michael had been in his early twenties at the time, not inclined towards Freemasonry himself, but he had been happy to serve as his father's practice audience as Maciek explained how the Temple, and the Tabernacle before it, shown in the green-colored handout, were esoteric symbols of the path of spiritual development.

The last of the sunshine crept up past the diagram for Maciek's talk. A line of shadow followed, darkening first the bottom of the illustration, then the middle, as Michael watched, sitting on his father's bed with Millie's tree ornament in his hands. Just before the last of the light left the diagram, Michael stood up, turned on the overhead light, and took the frame down from the wall. "He spoke from a text," Michael said to himself as he pulled the shades down to keep out the night. Then he went digging through boxes of his father's Masonic artifacts and writings.

By late that night, he had discovered his father's manuscript. He read of how the altar of burnt offerings symbolized the seeker's personal sacrifice, perhaps his sacrifice of means or time devoted to the spiritual quest, perhaps his divesting himself of those things of the world that weighed him down. He learned again that the laver symbolized purification, inside and out, in preparation for entering the domain of the spiritual, symbolized by the inner enclosure. Entering the enclosure at the Holy Place symbolized the spiritual world, and it was a domain of light—light from the golden menorah— where the chosen people were always kept in mind before the Divine: the twelve loaves of showbread on their table. The altar of incense was a place of prayer. The Most Holy Place— what men called the Holy of Holies, the Inner Sanctum—was the place of the Divine Presence Itself, where the Ark of the Covenant held the sacred relics of the chosen people's history: the stone tablets of the law, Aaron's rod that had budded, the pot of manna. The top of the Ark, the Mercy Seat with its two cherubim, was the Divine Throne whence God communed with the prophet, and where the high priest atoned for sin.

Michael made a list of the materials he would collect, and another of the tasks he had to fulfill.

By dawn, Michael had eaten, washed, and dressed, and had retrieved his post-hole digger from the garage. Fortunately, it was predicted to be an unseasonably cool day.

WEST

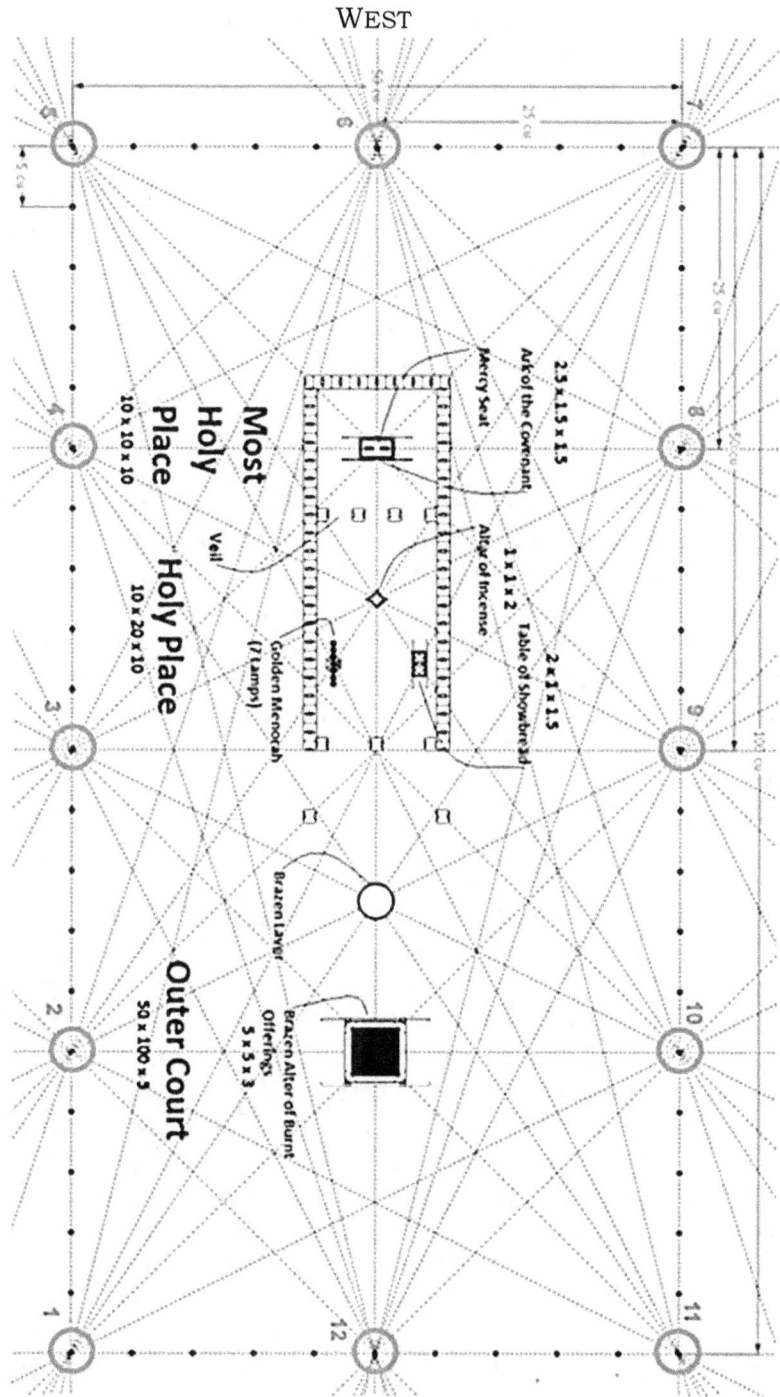

Ark of the Covenant
2.5 x 1.5 x 1.5

Mercy Seat

Most
Holy
Place
10 x 10 x 10

Veil

'Holy Place
10 x 20 x 10

Golden Menorah
(7 Lamps)

Altar of Incense
1 x 1 x 2

Table of Showbread
2 x 1 x 1.5

Brazen Laver

Outer Court
50 x 100 x 5

Brazen Alter of Burnt
Offerings
5 x 5 x 3

Michael was not about to dig sixty post holes, like those needed for the sockets of the fence of the outer court of the Tabernacle. He would dig twelve for the main supports of the outer court, and then four for the corners of the inner enclosure. Michael was blessed with a lot of space on the back of his property, so he had space for a hundred-cubit-long (or one-hundred-fifty-feet-long) outer court. With no neighbors left residing on adjoining properties, he had plenty of privacy.

With the spare lumber in his garage, Michael had his posts in before most folks in town had gotten to breakfast. Then it was off to his properties.

The Empty Quarter of Poughkeepsie had once been full of people, many of whom had rented properties from Michael. As these houses and apartments became vacant, Michael never bothered to clear out perhaps a quarter of them, hoping to rent them as furnished spaces. It was to these properties that he went with a pickup truck.

All along Lebanon Road he went from house to apartment to house, collecting bed sheets, sheets upon sheets, until the back of his pickup looked like he ran a laundry. He also collected a few light articles of furniture, a couple of end tables, a hope chest, and some knick-knacks.

At noon, he called Tom to see how everyone was holding up. There had been no change in Millie's condition. Penelope was numb, and Tom was no better. Michael promised to meet them for dinner at the hospital.

The better part of the afternoon Michael spent stringing up sheets on clotheslines from post to post in his back yard, to form the walls of the Outer Court and the enclosure of his tabernacle. For the walls of the Most Holy Place, Michael used some velvet sheets he had found here and there, scarlet, blue, some gold for the western wall. For the veil separating the Holy Place from the Most Holy Place, he used sheets that the little Johnson boy had left behind in his family's apartment: astronomy-themed sheets, with stars and planets and comets superimposed on the darkness of outer space. He moved in a few small articles of furniture, and went off to meet Tom and Penelope at the hospital.

Tom said that the doctors had begun to detect an increase in pressure in Millie's spinal fluid. They had expected this to happen, and were taking further countermeasures.

They had begun treatment with two antibiotics that had just received government approval the month before, medications so new that they had to be delivered to the hospital by courier from the manufacturer. It was possible that these drugs might work where other medications had failed. *Or not,* Michael thought. One way or the other, although this night too would likely be quiet, the next day would be a time of crisis.

As Tom explained all this to Michael in the hospital cafeteria, Michael saw that Penelope pushed peas around her plate as if she might eat them one day. Tom was just two steps short of zombiehood himself. When a clumsy hospital visitor accidentally jostled Tom with a tray, Tom repeated the last two sentences he had spoken exactly as he'd said them before the jostle, and then continued along, as if he clung to a script for the sake of preserving his sanity. Michael had never seen his son or his daughter-in-law in such distress.

Michael drove behind Tom and Penelope to their home. When they arrived, he sat Tom down in a chair in the middle of their living room, a spacious room full of pictures of Millie and her parents. Michael stood behind Tom, placed his hands on Tom's head, and said, "Thomas Michael Kozak, by the power and authority of the Melchizedek priesthood, which I bear, I place my hands upon your head and give you a father's blessing ...." Afterwards, Penelope sat in that chair while Tom gave her a husband's blessing, assisted by Michael.

Tom and Penelope slept very soundly that night. Michael spent about two hours making triple-sized corn muffins and cleaning up, then he, too, slept deeply, though not as long.

Michael's tabernacle was set far back from the house, and off to one side, so the rays of the rising sun hit the tabernacle's entrance early on. Michael came out of his house right at dawn, dressed all in white, from his jacket and tie down to his shoes. It was a suit he had worn inside the Latter-day Saint Temple in Manhattan, seventy miles to the south, back when he used to attend temple worship. Michael pulled along with him an old luggage cart, which squeaked as it rolled into the Outer Court of the tabernacle, past Post #12.

Twenty-five cubits, or about 38 feet, west of the entrance to the Outer Court stood a fifty-gallon drum that stood in for the altar of burnt offerings. The drum already had newspaper and wood chips in the bottom for kindling. Michael tossed in some charcoal briquettes, spritzed it all with lighter fluid, threw in a lighted match, and stepped quickly out of the way of the small fireball that he anticipated would erupt. He covered the drum with some salvaged barbecue grillwork.

Michael reached into the box on the luggage cart and pulled out the five parts of *The Book of Michael*, one volume at a time. He stuffed the pages of each volume between the grillwork to the flames about half an inch of sheets at a time. In minutes, he had fed all the pages to the flames. The empty binders went back into the box. Michael placed some sturdy fine mesh between the top of the drum and the barbecue grill to keep the ashes inside.

A few paces west of the drum, a ceramic birdbath once belonging to the late Gasparo Romero, a former tenant of Michael's, was set up to stand in for the laver. Michael took two gallon jugs of water from the box on the luggage cart, filled the birdbath/laver, hung his jacket on the luggage cart, rolled up his sleeves, removed his tie, and washed and wiped the smell of the soot out of his face and his hands. He had already showered that morning, but he washed his arms and face as if he were washing off, not just the soot, not just the words that had become the soot, but the years of pain and grievance and grudge that were behind those words. Finally he reached for the towel that was in the box and dried off his arms and face; his shoulders shook as he hid his face, and he held the towel there for a long time. He put the towel away, rolled down his sleeves, retied his necktie, and put on his jacket again. He wheeled the luggage cart to the entryway of the Holy Place, and left it outside.

From the cart, he took twelve large corn muffins. (This was the only item that Michael knew how to bake.) He placed the corn muffins on the table of showbread—Consuelo Rivera's former coffee table—at the north wall of the Holy Place, and as he placed each oversized muffin on the table, he said the name of a member of his family, beginning with Millie in the southwest corner of the table (closest to the Most Holy Place), and ending with himself at the northeast corner.

Along the south wall of the Holy Place stood an actual, if inexpensive, brass menorah, left behind when Saul Rabinowitz's kids closed out his apartment when he died. Using a lighter, Michael lit each of the seven candles of the menorah. With the candles lighted, Michael just stood for a while between the menorah and the table of the showbread, facing west.

Michael walked to the altar of incense, once known as the D'Amicos' metal candy bowl, atop Mr. D'Amico's nightstand; he lit a stick of sandalwood incense with his lighter. Michael had placed Mrs. Katkowski's prie-dieu kneeler there, and he knelt and prayed as the smoke of the incense floated up.

He asked forgiveness for having wasted his life in resentment. He confessed his unworthiness to ask for any favor from heaven. And, because he had come to do precisely that, he asked forgiveness in advance for his presumption.

Michael got up from the altar of incense, parted the veil made of young Master Johnson's outer-space-themed sheets, parted the wall made by Carlotta MacKenzie's golden velvet bed sheets, and entered the Most Holy Place.

At the hospital, the pressure on Millie's brain was increasing. The doctors sent Tom and Penelope out of Millie's isolation room to the waiting area. Penelope and Tom sat and held each other and gently cried while the nurses prepared Millie to be moved to an operating room.

Tom knelt on a piece of shag carpeting, before the Ark of the Covenant and the Mercy Seat. For an Ark, Michael had Ms. MacKenzie's hope chest, left behind with her golden velvet sheets when she skipped out on the rent, some years ago. The Ark now held articles that meant family to Michael: his father Maciek's Masonic medals, some pieces of his mother's wedding china, pictures of his children and grandchildren, Millie's Christmas ornament.

Atop the Ark was the Mercy Seat, a heavy glass table-top of Mr. Rabinowitz's that fit nicely atop Ms. Mackenzie's hope chest. Atop the table-top Michael had placed Mrs. DeVito's two plaster Renaissance angels, male and female—reproductions she'd gotten at the shop of the Metropolitan Museum of Art—to stand in for cherubim.

Michael knelt before this all in the Most Holy Place. The sun was now high enough in the sky to illuminate the scene through the thin white bedsheets that formed the roof of Michael's version of the Holy of Holies. For a moment, Michael took this all in and saw it as what, on one level of reality, it actually was.

How utterly pathetic, he thought. Mismatched pieces of dead people's furniture; bed sheets torn from the broken dreams of a half-dozen tattered lives. This was his Holy of Holies. He hung his head in shame and closed his eyes.

He remembered his father trying to teach him some kabbalistic wisdom, after another of his Masonic lectures, so long ago. "There are many levels of reality," Maciek had said, "and what we do on our level reverberates through them all, for good or evil. Any act of good, any act of sacrifice, however humble, makes a difference."

Michael opened his eyes. *Well, at least I've got the humble part down right*, he thought.

His knees were hurting, and the diabetic neuropathy in his feet made them throb. Michael had anticipated that this would happen, so he had placed a chair in the corner of the Most Holy Place. He repositioned the chair onto the carpet, and sat.

His plans had run out right about here. What was he going to say to God?

Ask Him to heal Millie, of course. But why should He? Because Michael would promise to live differently forever afterward, rejoin the human race, be a better father and grandfather and brother within his own family? But Michael should just do that anyway. No leverage there.

Michael could not think of any special great deeds he could do. Even if he could, was God to be bribed?

Finally, Michael decided that what he could offer was acceptance. If Millie lived, he would be the grandfather he was supposed to be, a loving presence in her life. If Millie died, he would be the father and father-in-law he was supposed to be, helping Tom and Penelope to navigate the terrible storm that was the death of a child. Either way, he'd be a bigger part of the lives of all his family. This is what Michael prayed, a request and an offering of submission, not a bribe.

It was getting hot and humid, not at all like the day before. Michael became drowsy. The last shreds of the *Book of Michael* went crisp within the Altar of Burnt Offerings.

Michael stood in the ancient Most Holy Place, in the Temple built by Solomon. The gleaming golden cherubim were clenched in a sacred embrace. Cuts in the stone high up on the wall let in light that reflected off all the gold in the room, bathing everything in a soft glow. Above the Mercy Seat was—what? Nothing that could be seen, at least not now. But the room was full of a Presence that Michael felt was centered in that spot. In the distance, Michael heard the sound of tinkling bells growing louder, and he know these were the tiny bells shaped like pomegranates on the hem of the robe of the high priest. Suddenly the bells stopped, and someone behind Michael said, "It is time."

His mobile phone woke Michael up. It was Tom calling. "I'll be right there," Michael said, and then he ran outside.

The next day, Michael started to disassemble his tabernacle, starting with the Most Holy Place. He found places for the components of the Ark of the Covenant in his home, as he did for a few other articles; Mr. Rabinowitz's menorah would provoke puzzled glances from visitors to Michael's home for years. He washed and donated all the sheets to a charity thrift store, where he ignored the raised eyebrows of the donation clerks as they looked over all those velvet sheets.

A few weeks after most everything was cleared away, Michael put up a swing set that he purchased, with seven sets of swings. When Millie asked about this, Michael explained that this was for when she visited with her cousins. That made sense to her, and she hopped off the swing to look at the birds in the bird bath. Michael followed, his hands in his pockets.

Acknowledgements

Some of the stories in this collection first appeared, in different form, in online literary magazines:

- "The Cryptographer" in *Foliate Oak Literary Magazine* (where the original story was dedicated to Ms. Denise Sutherland, cryptogram expert *extraordinaire*).

- "The Gondolier of Bethesda Landing" in *The Fear of Monkeys.*

- "The Death of Mozart" in *The Legendary.*

I thank Danny Goodman and my fellow students at Gotham Writers Workshop for their thoughtful comments on some of these stories, and for their encouragement.

I am particularly grateful to the late Marilyn T. Pease, Ph.D., who supervised my independent study in creative writing at Regis High School in New York City, 1973-1974. Dr. Pease was an exemplary teacher who cared a great deal for her students, including one scruffy kid from the Lower East Side. I like to think that she would be pleased to see these humble offerings, which I dedicate to her memory.

— MEK-R

Illustration Credits

Note: All URL links were current as of the date of publication. All images in the black-and-white edition have been modified from the color originals.

Cover Image: This is a modification of an image of an alley in downtown Olympia, Washington. The original image was made in March 2007 by Joe Mabel, and appears here under the terms of the GNU Free Documentation License, Version 1.2 or later. The image was downloaded from http://commons.wikimedia.org/wiki/File:Oly_alley_01.jpg

Page vii: This is a modification of a detail of a Hammonds map, "New York City and Vicinity," originally published in 1906. The image is in the public domain, and was downloaded from http://en.wikipedia.org/wiki/File:1906_NYC_vicinity_map.jpg

Page viii: This is a modification of a map (New York State—Central Park quadrangle) obtained from the website of the United States Geological Survey, an agency of the U.S. Department of the Interior. The original image is in the public domain.

Page ix: This is a modification of a map (New York State—Brooklyn quadrangle) obtained from the website of the United States Geological Survey, an agency of the U.S. Department of the Interior. The original image is in the public domain. The misspelling of "Gramercy" is in the original.

Facing Page 1: This is a detail of an image of the sun, showing the horizon of the Earth. The original image was created by a spacewalking astronaut during STS-134, the last spaceflight of U.S Space Shuttle *Endeavor*, on May 27, 2011. The original image is in the public domain because it was created by NASA. The image was downloaded from http://en.wikipedia.org/wiki/File:STS-134_EVA4_view_to_the_Russian_Orbital_Segment.jpg

Page 12: This is a modification of an image of a reproduction of a Confederate Cypher Disk on display in the National Cryptologic Museum at Fort Meade, Maryland. The original image was made in October, 2010, by the Wikipedia user "RadioFan," and appears here under the terms of the Creative Commons

Page 56: This is an image of the plan of Jezreel's Tower, formerly in Gillingham, Kent, England. (The tower was partially built in the 1880s; the plan, if dating to that time, would be in the public domain, as would any images of it, according to American copyright law.) The image is attributed to Cunningham at the English language Wikipedia, and appears here under the GNU Free Documentation License, Version 1.2 or later, and the Creative Commons Attribution-Share Alike 3.0 Unported license. The image was uploaded to Wikipedia by Cunningham on April 6, 2006, and was downloaded from http://commons.wikimedia.org/wiki/File:Jeztow3.jpg

Page 64: This is a detail of an image of melted Crayola™ crayon artwork, uploaded to the Internet by the author, "Townzerz," and dated October 10, 2011. The image appears here under the Creative Commons Attribution-Share Alike 3.0 Unported license. The image was downloaded from http://commons.wikimedia.org/wiki/File:Melted_crayons.JPG

Page 70: This is a detail of the image on page 81.

Page 81: This author modified and annotated an image of the Tabernacle found on the website, http://theholyhouse.org

About the Author

Mark Koltko-Rivera was born and raised in the East Village, on the Lower East Side of Manhattan. He has lived for substantial periods of time in Hiroshima, Japan; the suburbs of Philadelphia; inner-city Newark, New Jersey; and Central Florida. He currently lives in New York City.

At various times in his life, Koltko-Rivera has worked as a janitor, hardware store stock clerk, security officer, LDS (Mormon) missionary, systems analyst, director of marketing, psychotherapist, college and graduate school instructor, and as a director of research. For a brief period as a pre-teen, he worked unknowingly as a numbers runner.

He has appeared as an expert in documentaries broadcast on the *Discovery* and *History* channels, and has acted in episodes of the online TV series, *Math Warriors*. He is a graduate of Haverford College, Fordham University, and New York University.

His fiction has appeared in several online literary magazines. Three other stories of his appear as interlocking narratives, all encrypted, in *Cracking Codes and Cryptograms for Dummies®* (co-authored with Denise Sutherland; Wiley, 2010).

Koltko-Rivera is at work on a variety of literary projects, fiction and nonfiction, including works for the stage and screen. Readers may learn more about these projects at the author's website: www.markkoltko-rivera.com .

He can be found at the "Mark Koltko-Rivera, Writer" page on Facebook.

His Twitter feed is available at @MarkKoltkoRiver .

The author receives e-mail at: authorMEKR@yahoo.com .